Horseman

Book I - The Awakening

By A. Kairos

First published by Dark Protocol Publication 2025

First edition

ISBN *(paperback):* 979-8-9932772-0-2
ISBN *(hardcover):* 979-8-9932772-1-9

For my family,
whose love has carried me through every storm.
For Jess,
my heart, my anchor, my forever.

Contents

Preface

Stories are born from shadows. Some linger in the back of the mindlike whispers carried on cold stone, waiting to be spoken aloud. This one has followed me for years. in quiet hours, in restless dreams, in the silence between heartbeats.

It began with a single image: a prison hidden beneath a monastery, and within it, something chained that was never meant to be found. From that moment, the story grew, weaving itself through fragments of faith, myth, and the frailty of human choice.

This book is not just pages bound in ink. It is a journey through judgment, sacrifice, and the weight of love when the world darkens around it. My hope is that, as you walk these halls with Jessica and meet the shadows waiting there, you feel what I felt when I first gave this story breath.

Every word here was written with the love and strength of those who stand beside me. To my family, who gave me the courage to follow this voice into the dark. And to Jess. My heart, whose faith has carried me farther than I ever dreamed. The story is yours now. Step inside.

Acknowledgments

No story is ever written alone. This book. and the long nights behind it. would not exist without the unwavering love and support of those around me.

To my friends and mentors who offered encouragement when I needed it most. your words reminded me that stories matter, even when the path feels uncertain.

And to the readers. those who step willingly into these shadows and give life to the characters I could only imagine . this book is for you as much as it is from me. May you find something here that lingers with you, long after the final page is turned.

Please leave a review @
amazon.com/author/akairos_horseman_official

Prologue. From the Journal of Brother Adam

The Final Year of My Charge

I set down these words because silence has grown heavier than speech.

When the Abbot placed the iron ring of keys in my hand, he called it "a simple trust." I was young enough to think obedience could be simple. We stood in the winter cloister where the stones breathe cold through the soles of your feet, and he told me I would keep watch over the **Sanctuary Wing**, that long corridor no one crosses after Compline, where the dust settles deeper than prayer. "You will check the locks," he said, "keep the records, and ask no questions."

I asked them anyway, but only to myself.

The elders. those with voices like dry vellum. called the place **the sealed wing**. They never said more than they needed. Only stray fragments slipped through their teeth: "the nameless one" … "the damned one" … "what our fathers buried so that we might be allowed to live under heaven." I was told this once and never again. It is a hard lesson, to be told a thing once and be expected to carry it for a lifetime.

I walked in that hall each night. The iron studs of the doors were cold under my palm. My lamp smoked; my breath smoked; even my thoughts felt like smoke. I recorded what could be measured. rust flaking from hinges, mortar that wept with damp, a draft that came and went with the moon. but not the part that pressed at the ribs, the sense that the place remembered more than it wished to say.

The Accident

If there is a sin worse than disobedience, it is curiosity that pretends to be duty.

The monastery had been built to keep the world out.
Or perhaps to keep something in.

Its stones were old, quarried from the mountains before any of the monks had been born, before even their fathers' fathers. Every corridor smelled of damp earth and candle wax, every prayer seemed to vanish into the silence without echo. To live here was to forget time itself.

And yet, for all its stillness, the monks built. They built the library. a vast hall of rising shelves, of iron locks and hidden alcoves, of staircases that wound up into shadows. They built it not for themselves but for the centuries to come, a treasury of memory and scripture, a safeguard against forgetting.

Brother Adam was meant to be a builder of books, a keeper of silence. But curiosity clung to him like a second skin. When his brothers slept, he lingered over old parchments until the oil in his lamp burned low. When they prayed, his mind wandered into questions that the Psalms never answered. And when he walked the unfinished halls, he listened to the stones, as though they might whisper secrets through their mortar.

One night, his curiosity betrayed him.

He had gone searching in the sealed wing, where the stone was darker, the air sharper, as if the mountain itself disapproved of his presence. His lantern rattled against the wall as he stumbled over a broken flagstone, light spilling too far down the corridor. That was when he saw it. not scripture, not relic, not stone.

A figure.

At first, he thought it was a statue abandoned in the dark. Gaunt and thin, the body was bound upright by chains as thick as a man's wrist. Their links glowed faintly, etched with runes that pulsed like embers dying in ash.

And then there was the helmet.

Forged of black iron and marked with glyphs too precise to be the work of men, it sealed the prisoner's head completely. No visor, no seam, no clasp. Only the jaw was left exposed, a gaunt line of bone, lips dry but unmistakably alive. Sightless, airless. impossible. and yet Adam saw the faint rise and fall of breath.

Fear rooted him where he stood. Every instinct screamed to flee. Yet he returned.
First out of terror, then out of fascination, and then because he could not stop himself.

The prisoner spoke. His voice was muffled, hollow through the helmet, but it carried. low, resonant, the kind of voice that filled the chamber without ever rising above a whisper. And Adam, who should have run, who should have confessed to his brothers, instead stayed and listened.

And he wrote.

At first it was scraps on parchment. Then full journals, thick with names and places he had never known cities lost to fire, empires rising and collapsing, rivers that had run red and deserts that had swallowed armies. The man remembered everything, and Adam recorded it all.

Years passed. The shelves of the library grew taller. So too did the secret shelves Adam filled with his forbidden work. The monks thought him devout, lost in ceaseless transcription. They never knew that every night he descended to speak with the chained man, to ask, to listen, to write.

The prisoner never asked to be freed. Only remembered.

By the end of Adam's life, his hands trembled with every stroke of the quill. His hair was white, his back bent, but still he came, night after night, candle flame in one hand, ink in the other. His journals filled an alcove of their own. a hidden library inside the greater one.

And then, on a winter evening, Adam felt his end near. His lamp burned low, frost clung to the corners of his cell, and his breath came shallow. Still, he sat at his desk, bent over parchment.

His quill scratched a final entry:

"If any should find these words, know I did not write them for fear nor for faith alone, but for truth. The man below is not simply man. His chains are carved with judgment, his helm forged by hands not mortal. I have seen his sorrow. I have heard his wrath. He is no statue, no myth. He is the shadow beneath heaven itself."

The ink blotched. His vision dimmed. But with one last surge of will, he scratched a name onto the parchment. the name the prisoner had spoken, muffled through iron, heavy with meaning.

"James."

The quill slipped from his hand. His head bowed as though in prayer. Brother Adam's breath slowed, then stopped. He passed quietly at his desk, surrounded by shelves that would outlive him.

The library endured. His words endured.
And in the darkness below, the prisoner still waited.

Closing the Book

I have written more than I should. It is evening. The wind finds every seam in these old walls and plays the same few notes until the stone hums with them. The brothers, those who remain sleep or remember how to. I have set the keys where a man with clean hands may find them, and I have placed these pages where a man with a clean heart might be tempted to read them.

It comforts me to pretend that the work is finished because we have become few. I can write that the seals have held, that the shelves have made forgetfulness easier than remembrance, that the names we were told to shun have been emptied of power by disuse. I can say, with the beautiful lie good men tell themselves at the end of a long task, that **all this has passed**.

I can even write, as the elders would prefer, in the **past tense**.

But paper is more honest than its author.

I will end as a witness, not as a scribe.

His name is James… and he *is* damned.

Chapter 1. The Routine

The alarm stirred Jessica Trainer awake before dawn, the faint glow of 5:00 a.m. numbers blinking against the dark of her Langley, Virginia apartment. She rolled out of bed with a methodical practiced ease, the quiet of the early hour wrapping around her like an old friend. A mug of coffee was always first, black, strong, with enough creamer and sugar to sweeter her tongue, and hot enough to wake her bones. Steam rose against her face as she leaned against the counter, the warmth grounding her before the day began.

At 5:15 a.m., Jessica was at the gym. Cardio first, pounding out miles on the treadmill, then weights, her form precise, her rhythm steady. Sweat trickled down her temples, her breathing controlled, her body moving like clockwork. By the time she hit the showers, she felt the heaviness of sleep burn away. Dressed and pressed, she slid into her black jacket and gun harness, her firearm snug against her side, braids fixed neatly back. By 8:00 a.m., she was at her cubicle, her workday beginning the way it always did. files, leads, paperwork, and silence.

Her life was a cycle of repetition; one she wore like armor.

The next morning was different. She woke earlier than usual, being restless, she sat up and pushed her legs to the side of the bed. Then stood up making her way to her closer, she changed into her workout attire, and laced her shoes, and slipped outside into the still-quiet streets of Langley. The air was crisp with the faint scent of freshly baked bread drifting from a corner bakery. Market vendors stirred to life, shuffling crates and calling to one another as the first rays of dawn stretched over the horizon. Jessica settled into her run, zoning out the world, letting the steady rhythm of her strides and the beat of her pulse guide her.

The neighborhood was still half-asleep. The smell of bread drifted from a bakery a few blocks away, early vendors shuffled crates of produce into place, and the horizon was only beginning to bleed orange and pink. She found herself slipping into a rare calm, zoning out the noise of the world as her feet struck pavement, every stride steady, controlled.

When she reached headquarters, she paused. From outside she could see the looming glass and steel of the building, her eyes rising toward the fifth floor. her floor. In just a few short hours, that cubicle would swallow her whole again. But not yet.

She swiped her badge and descended into the sub-basement training wing. Down here, the Bureau kept everything. tactical courses, combat instructors, classrooms, sparring rings. This was her sanctuary.

She slipped into the boxing class she favored. Taylor, the grizzled old-school instructor, gave her a nod as she wrapped her hands.

"You're late," he barked, voice gravelly.

"I'm early everywhere else," Jessica shot back, driving her fists into the heavy bag with sharp, precise strikes. Sweat rolled down her brow as her knuckles thudded against leather. Taylor barked corrections, always pushing her harder, but she thrived under his watch. Here, she wasn't an analyst, or an agent bound to casework and screens. In this place here she was just herself.

From boxing, she crossed into the indoor range. Her weapon came alive in her hands, the recoil a rhythm she knew by heart. Round after round punched through the paper target, her shot groups tight, centered. The range officer gave her a curt nod of approval, nothing more, but enough to tell her she was still sharp.

The showers in the training wing weren't her favorite. too sterile, too industrial. but the water was hot, and that was all she needed. She let it wash the sweat away, steam billowing around her as she stared at herself in the mirror afterward. Her coat hung nearby, alongside her shoulder harness with her standard-issue firearm tucked inside. She fixed her braids into their everyday pattern, buckled the harness, slipped on the pressed jacket, and adjusted her collar until every line was crisp. Jessica Trainer always looked professional. and she intended to keep it that way.

Before heading upstairs, she made her usual stop at the downstairs coffee stand. The aroma of fresh grounds mingled with the chatter of agents cutting through the lobby. She ordered her cup, then. of course. Agent Randall was there, leaning against the counter with his trademark smirk.

"Morning, Trainer," he said, tilting his cup toward her. "One of these days, you're going to say yes. Coffee? Dinner? Hell, I'll even settle for cafeteria lunch. Sixty whole minutes of your undivided attention."

Jessica rolled her eyes, suppressing a smile. Randall wasn't bad-looking, and he wasn't a bad agent either. but he was a try-hard. Charming, slightly arrogant, always chasing what he couldn't have.

"Not today, Randall." She raised her cup in mock salute. "Or tomorrow."

"Ah, so you're saying there's hope for Friday?" he shot back.

She shook her head and walked off, his exaggerated groan echoing behind her.

"One of these days, Trainer! You'll see. I'm wearing you down!"

By the time she reached her cubicle on the fifth floor, she was still smirking to herself. But the smirk faded as her monitor lit with a new email.

The subject line froze her:

"Are you coming to Rome???"

Her breath caught. The name stirred something deeper. Henry Worthington III. Mentor. Old partner. The man who had trained her, guided her, and kept her steady when the Bureau tried to grind her down. She clicked it open.

From: Henry.Worthington@securecomms.int
To: Jessica.Trainer@cia.gov
Subject: Are you coming to Rome???

Jessica,

It's been too long. I'll keep this short because I know how much you hate long emails. We've got a situation here in Rome, a very strange one this time. Not our normal case work as we have had in the past, this one goes back historically further beyond anything we have seen.

There's an old monastery here in Rome. Turns out, part of it shares its foundation with **Atticus Prison**. One of the prison wings had inmates falling sick. not from anything contagious, but when workers came to clean the ventilation system, they found something. You'll have to see it for yourself.

Before the Bureau sends in their own teams to lock this place down, our job is simple:

- Security check.
- Ensure the inmates don't have access to the tunnels.
- Close out any old chambers.
- And make sure the monks still have a safe place of worship.

It's dark, it's dirty...you'll love it.

"Oh, my dear Henry" she said to herself as she stopped reading further.

Jessica leaned back in her chair, the corners of her lips tugging upward despite herself.

"The only dark, dirty thing is you, Henry," she muttered, chuckling to herself under her breath.

Coffee in hand, she stared at the glowing email a moment longer, her pulse quickening with an anticipation she hadn't felt in months. Rome. Henry. A monastery tied to a prison. It was different. and different was exactly what she needed.

Her routine had just been broken.

And nothing would ever be the same again.

Chapter 2. The Arrival and Old Friends

The morning Jessica left Virginia; the sky was muted with an overcast haze. The kind that seemed to press down on the city, dulling every sound. She sat by the airport window with a coffee in hand, watching planes taxi across the tarmac, their lights cutting faintly through the mist. Her carry-on rested by her leg, her service pistol tucked safely away, holstered and discreet, the weight of it grounding her even as her world shifted.

The announcement for boarding echoed, a hollow, metallic voice calling her row. She rose, smoothing her jacket, the braid at her back still damp from her early morning shower. She'd gone through her routine one final time at Langley before leaving. gym at dawn, heavy bag, a few rounds at the range. knowing it would be weeks before she could return to the normal cadence of her days.

On the plane, she tucked herself against the window, letting the hum of the engines drown her thoughts. She pressed her hand against the glass as the runway blurred, D.C.'s skyline shrinking, swallowed by clouds. A strange calm settled over her. For the first time in years, she wasn't bound to the monotony of reports and cubicles. For the first time, she was being pulled into something unknown.

She opened her tablet, the glow of the screen lighting her features, and scrolled to the message. Henry Worthington III. her old mentor, the man who had once guided her through her early years in the bureau. His words had pulled her from her comfortable orbit. She read the email again, slowly this time, letting each line press into her mind.

Jessica continued to read the email form where she had previously left off, a new profound interest pulling her curiosity to know what else he had to say about this case.

Its dark, dirty...you'll love it

The details of this case are peculiar, but also very standard, your involvement will be secondary as I will be the lead in this case.

We've come across something strange here in Rome. A prison. *Atticus Prison.* that shares a foundation with the ruins of an old monastery. During maintenance in one of the wings, workers became ill when clearing the ventilation shafts. They uncovered something unusual, something best seen with your own eyes.

The elders here whisper of a "Nameless One," the *damned one.* Folklore, perhaps. But what I've seen... it demands a closer look. Our task is simple before headquarters sends their own teams: ensure inmates cannot access the old tunnels, seal any exposed chambers, and guarantee the monks have a safe place of worship.

It should be little more than a security inspection. But there's history on these walls, Jessica. History no one here seems eager to speak of. I await your arrival.

Sincerely with love,

Henry Worthington III

Jessica smirked despite herself, shaking her head. "The only dark and dirty thing is you, Henry," she said aloud once more, this time earning a quick chuckle from the woman seated across the aisle. Jessica ignored her, tucking the tablet away, but her amusement faded as her mind circled the words again. *Nameless one. Damned one.*

The engines roared as the plane cut through the clouds and carried her across the Atlantic. She pulled her jacket closer around her shoulders, leaning back into the seat. Sleep wouldn't come, only the restless shifting between memories and the questions Henry's email had carved into her.

Hours later, Rome rose into view beneath the descending plane, bathed in gold from the setting sun. The ancient city spread out like a tapestry of stone and history, the dome of St. Peter's Basilica gleaming in the distance. Jessica pressed her forehead against the glass, a quiet breath leaving her lips. For all her years of chasing cases across states, across borders, she had never been to Italy.

As the wheels struck the runway, a jolt ran through her body. half anticipation, half unease.

The terminal doors sighed open, and Rome's early evening pressed against her like a warm palm: air the temperature of old stone, tinged with jet fuel, espresso, and sea-salt from somewhere she couldn't see. Italian and English overlapped in the arrivals hall, the cadence of one language softening the edges of the other. People waved, cried, argued lovingly. Jessica adjusted the strap of her carry-on and scanned: exits, choke points, faces, posture. Habit. always habit.

The terminal was a blur of faces and fluorescent light, a restless tide of travelers weaving through customs lines and luggage belts. Jessica adjusted the satchel strap on her shoulder, its weight grounding her, and scanned the crowd.

"Jess."

The voice cut through the din. She turned.

Henry stood near a pillar beneath the sign for ground transport, two paper cups in hand. His hair was more silver than she remembered, but his smile was the same as it had always been when she saw him last, that mix of mischief and warmth that managed to disarm her even after years apart.

"I brought coffee," he said, lifting the cups like a peace offering. "And before you accuse me of sabotage, this one I had ordered especially for you my dear."

She arched a brow, skeptical, but took the cup anyway. The heat bled through her palms, promising comfort. She took a grateful sip and gagged almost immediately. The taste was molten asphalt. Bitter, black, scalding.

"Henry!!"

He blinked, then laughed, unashamed. "Oh, right! that's mine." He swapped cups so fast she barely processed it, his grin widening. The side eye she gave him was unmistakable, but she tasted the second cup, before she spoke. The second was sweeter, cream softening the edge, exactly the way she liked it.

Jessica glared at him over the lid, but her lips betrayed her with the twitch of a smile.

"You did that on purpose."

"Best laugh I've had all week," he said, unapologetic.

"Only because you enjoy my suffering."

"I enjoy your presence," he corrected softly, and for a moment the noise of the terminal faded, leaving just the weight of his words between them.

Jessica looked away first, brushing her braid back over her shoulder. "Let's just get out of the airport before you decide to poison me again."

Henry chuckled and clapped her shoulder, steering her toward the exit. "Deal. But I'm holding onto the bitter stuff. Builds character."

They threaded through the crush, out to the taxi ranks where horns chorused and luggage wheels rattled like castanets. He led her to a black Alfa with dings on the doors and the resigned dignity of a car that had survived a city. When the engine turned over, the radio crackled with a mournful ballad, and Henry lowered the windows. Rome poured in.

Traffic moved like water around stone. Vespas stitched between lanes, the riders talking with their hands at thirty miles an hour. Market stalls hung open like mouths. pyramids of peppers and tomatoes, baskets of figs, a fishmonger lifting a silver body to the light. The air kept changing masks: gasoline and basil, hot rubber and jasmine, wood smoke and baking bread.

"You look good," Henry said, glancing over from the driver's seat.

"So do you," she answered.

"Liar. You look good. I look like an archivist who lost a fight with time."

"You would have lost that fight twenty years ago."

He laughed, the sound bouncing in the small car. "Ah, there she is. My favorite critic."

They fell into their old rhythm. barb and counter barb, the comfort of knowing where the other would land. Between jokes, the city unfurled in tableaus: a fountain where children chased pigeons; a worn stone stair flanked by potted lemon trees; a courtyard where laundry drifted like surrendered flags. Church bells folded over the rooftops in slow, patient waves.

"Tell me again," she said, "about Atticus."

Henry's hands loosened on the wheel, then re-tightened. so faintly most people would miss it. "Later tonight," he said. "Once you're settled."

"That bad?"

"That layered." He glanced at her. "You've been on planes all day. And I promised you dinner."

~ 28 ~

They bypassed the city center and climbed toward higher ground where the streets narrowed, and vines swallowed walls. The monastery rose ahead, not grand so much as stubborn: stone on stone on stone, patched and re-patched, its silhouette cut clean against a bruised-purple sky. A bell tolled inside. one deep, resonant note that seemed to ripple the ivy.

The monastery rose out of the hills like something half-remembered from another age, its weathered stone walls kissed by ivy and shadow. By the time their car wound up the narrow road and pulled through the wrought-iron gate, the sun was beginning to slide low, casting long fingers of gold across the landscape.

Henry parked just shy of the steps, slipping out first before circling around to retrieve her bag. Jessica followed; her eyes locked on the façade. It wasn't just old. it was ancient, the kind of ancient that carried silence like a crown.

"Welcome to your new home away from home," Henry said, spreading his arms as if he were introducing a palace.

Jessica set her bag down on the first step, taking in the solemnity of the place. For the first time in weeks, her shoulders eased.

Inside, their footsteps echoed against marble floors as they passed rows of carved saints and painted frescos dulled by centuries. The Sanctuary Wing opened into a long corridor, every door polished, every handle untouched.

"This wing is private," Henry explained, stopping at the first chamber door. He leaned against the frame, lowering his voice as if the stones themselves might listen. "No one else occupies it. I think they prefer to keep us in solitude."

Jessica smirked, brushing past him with her bag. "Or keep us out of the way."

Their laughter bounced down the empty corridor like an old secret.

Henry pointed further. "My quarters are just there, should you need anything. Convenient, right? Though I'll warn you now. I don't snore, but I do talk in my sleep. You've been warned."

Jessica rolled her eyes. "Comforting."

"Oh, and before I forget. there are two locations. This one, and another flat in the city. Both are furnished, stocked, and available whenever we need them. That way we can work, or disappear, depending on the mood."

Jessica nodded, setting her bag on the narrow bed. The faint smell of incense lingered in the air, clinging to the old wooden beams. Solitude indeed.

Henry studied her with that teasing half-smile. "Maybe now you'll finally settle down. Find a man here in Rome, sweep you off your feet."

Jessica barked a short laugh. "Don't get your hopes up."

"Oh, I never lose hope," he quipped, straightening. "Now. freshen up. Then I'll take you into town. Show you the other place."

He stepped backward with a mock bow. "And afterward, dinner. I'm making my famous chicken Alfredo pasta."

Jessica raised a brow, skeptical. "You? Cooking?"

Henry pressed his hand dramatically to his chest, feigning offense. "Well… maybe I know a place I can pick it up from."

Jessica laughed, the sound breaking loose. Henry joined her, their voices echoing off the high stone arches until, for a moment, the monastery didn't feel empty at all.

TO THE CITY

By the time they reached the city flat, the sun had surrendered to twilight, Rome glowing in golden lamplight as scooters darted past and laughter spilled out of café doors. The air itself seemed to hum, fragrant with garlic and roasted meats, touched with the faint metallic tang of rain that had passed earlier in the day. The streets pulsed with movement. couples strolling hand in hand, shopkeepers drawing down awnings, children still running in packs, their shouts echoing in the alleys like birds scattering into dusk.

The flat sat on a quieter street, away from the louder avenues but still close enough to breathe in the city's heartbeat. It was a tall, stone-faced building whose windows stretched wide, trimmed in worn shutters painted green long ago, their edges now flaking to bare wood. Balconies curled out in iron vines, blackened by age but elegant still. Flower boxes spilled bright geraniums into the street below, their color burning even under the streetlamps.

Rome stretched in both directions, alive in twilight. Streetlamps painted the cobblestones in circles of fire. Scooters whined past like restless insects. The cafés nearby pulsed with life. cutlery clinking, glasses raised, voices layered in laughter and argument alike. A guitarist strummed beneath one of the lamps, his voice raw and imperfect, but passionate. An accordion wove through the tune, and together they made the air thrum with something old and intimate.

Jessica closed her eyes and inhaled. Garlic, roasting chestnuts, sweet pastries, the faint smoke of grilled meat, it all swirled together until she could taste the city itself.

It was nothing like the monastery. That silence had been weighty, suffocating, as though every stone pressed against her lungs. This silence as if it could be called silence. was alive, breathing. Vibrant.

Her shoulders loosened. She felt her spine straighten. For the first time in weeks, her professional armor cracked, and she felt herself stepping free. Here, she wasn't the operative, the shadow, the weapon. She was simply Jessica. Just a woman leaning over a railing, watching strangers live their small lives with laughter and light.

The realization both comforted and frightened her. She had grown so used to being studied, calculated, useful. Here, she could be wanted, unmeasured. The thought stirred something both sweet and restless deep inside.

She lingered there, imagining herself slipping into the current below. Walking among them, laughing without reason, touching without fear. A stranger among strangers, yet entirely free.

The thought warmed her.

The **flat** sat behind a wrought-iron gate that ivy had tried and failed to eat. Up three flights, past landings that smelled of lemon cleaner and dust, Henry unlocked a door and swept an arm. "Home number two."

The suite opened like a breath: tall windows with shutters ajar, floorboards that creaked honest notes, a little kitchen where copper pans glowed faintly, a living room scattered with books and maps as if someone had set up an argument and walked away mid-claim. A bedroom waited beyond with linen that looked like sleep instead of ceremony.

"Meet me in my room in one hour," Henry said, tilting his head toward the short hallway. It was delivered as orders softened by affection.

Jessica raised an eyebrow, half-amused, half-curious. "An hour?"

"Trust me." Henry winked. "Any less, you'll be late."

Shaking her head, Jessica stepped inside. The suite was larger than she expected. warm wooden floors, tall windows that breathed in the sounds of the city, and furniture too comfortable to have been meant for work. A full kitchen, a living room dressed in soft golden lamps, and beyond it a wide bedroom with an inviting bed draped in linen.

She dropped her bag on the counter, opened the refrigerator, and pulled out a bottled water. The cool condensation kissed her palm, a welcome relief after the day's climb of heat. For the first time, she let herself exhale deeply.

Night air shifted through the open shutters, brushing cool against her skin. Somewhere below, a car horn sounded, followed by the faint chorus of children's laughter spilling into the street. Rome was alive, and yet here in this flat, she was wrapped in stillness.

She started the shower. Steam filled the bathroom almost immediately, clinging to the mirror. She stripped away the day's layers, undoing the braid that had held her hair captive, and stepped under the spray. The water came hot, rolling down her body in soothing waves.

A moan slipped past her lips before she could stop it, the kind that came not from indulgence but from release. Every ache of travel, every ounce of tension melted under the steady cascade. She ran her fingers through her hair, letting the strands loosen and fall free over her shoulders.

"An hour?" she murmured aloud, smiling faintly to herself. "He should've given me three."

Reluctantly, she shut off the water, a silent promise forming in her mind to return later. For an indulgent second, she teased herself with the absurd fantasy of summoning the young bellhop she'd seen downstairs to join her and laughed at the ridiculousness of it. It felt good to laugh at nothing at all.

She toweled off, slipped into a soft dress the color of deep wine, and added simple jewelry that caught the lamplight in delicate glints. Her hair, now dry, curled easily into long elegant waves with a flick of the iron she always carried. In the mirror, she barely looked like the agent who had arrived that morning.

This Jessica was softer, polished, almost... alive in a way she rarely allowed herself to be.

She gave herself one last glance, nodded with quiet approval, and crossed the hall.

Knock. Knock.

Henry's voice carried through the door. "Come in."

Chapter 3. Threads in the Dark

The city glimmered beyond the floor-to-ceiling windows, a thousand pinpricks of light piercing the black night.
The air inside the Citadel's conference chamber was ionized, faintly metallic, like the moment before a lightning strike.

The oval table stretched wide, its black surface laced with swirling crimson patterns. At first glance, decorative and beautiful in design, until Markus' arrival would prove otherwise. The bosses had come one by one, each flanked by their own security details. The room smelled of expensive cologne, faint cigar smoke clinging to suits, the musk of leather from the chairs. Voices overlapped, over one another as quiet boasts of shipments moved, rivals eliminated, territories expanded, all chatter among them was syndicate business. Small displays of power among them traded like poker chips between wolves.

Near the far curve of the room, a little girl wandered barefoot along the glass. Her pale dress brushed her knees as she pressed her small hands to the window, tracing imaginary constellations from the city lights below. Her hair hung in loose waves, and when she glanced toward the table, her crystal blue eyes caught the light. flashing like sunlit ice. She giggled softly at something unseen, the sound pure yet lingering too long in the air. No one asked her to leave. No one dared. Only the head of the table was different. A space carved into the table to accommodate the man who had summoned them there, there was no need of a fine elaborate leather chair, just an empty gap precisely measured.

A soft chime, a whisper of hydraulics. Markus emerged from his private elevator. The first impression was of a frail, elderly man, not just elderly but ancient, and brittle, his facial hair was long but neatly trimmed beard of silver and white, thinning hair combed back. His skin was weathered parchment, the lines deep and unflinching. He wore a black suit cut to perfection, an ornate tie pin glinting under the lights, cufflinks catching the eye. His advanced auto-wheelchair moved without sound, gliding to his place at the head of the oval table.

He rested his hands on the table's edge, deep violet eyes sweeping the room, each gaze landing heavy, like a silent verdict. "There has been an awakening," Markus said softly. His voice was quiet, but it filled the chamber.

Vincent, seated midway down the right side, shifted into his chair. He leaned forward, tone dripping with arrogance in a deep Italian accent. "Markus, we've heard this before. Should we be throwing away our resources chasing fairy tales?"

Markus didn't look away. "I was speaking." The pause stretched, the very air tightening. Then he tilted his head. "But since you've interrupted, let me ask... Do you think the men in this chamber are loyal to you? Or, to me?"

Vincent's smirk and arrogance dropped immediately, and his voice fell silent. Markus' voice sharpened, a blade under silk. "I don't require your loyalty, or the loyalty of anyone in this room. I demand obedience and obedience without question. "

The swirling crimson within the table began to move, slow at first, then writhing like living smoke. No one dared breathe.

In the same instant, every guard in the room collapsed where they stood. No gasps, no struggle, just bodies collapsing like marionettes with cut strings. Blank expressions, followed with Hollow black sockets stared from their skulls where eyes had been seconds before. Silence now swallowed the chamber. Markus' gaze swept the table once more. "Find her. Use my assets to hunt her down."

He let the pause stretch; the silence heavy enough to press into bone.
"Send my Reapers. "It wasn't a suggestion, and he wasn't asking. It was a reminder to all around him, with the upmost subtly, but still layered heavy that everything in this room, every resource, every power, belonged to him and him alone.

Without another word, the massive screen at the far wall flickered to life. Jessica Trainer's profile filled the display, multiple images of her in public, dossier notes, known associates, and last confirmed locations as of twelve hours prior.

No one spoke. Not after what they'd just seen.

Markus leaned in on the table, "you have what you need, now go, I will not tolerate any failure, or excuses fairy tales or not." Markus looked directly at Vincent, as he swallowed nervously, rose from his seat and walked out with the others. No one spoke in the hallways or elevators down not their convoys.

The room cleared, and everyone left respectively, their guards meeting them at their elegantly parked vehicles, and their convoys left to set plans into motion using their networks and independent resources.

All except one member.

Vincent descended into the parking garage alone. His footsteps echoed between the concrete pillars, each step a hollow note in the cavernous dark. The air smelled faintly of oil, damp stone, and the metallic tang of rainwater dripping somewhere far off. His sedan waited in the far corner the blacked-out windows, sleek as a predator at rest.

 Two guards flanked the passenger side, exactly where they should be. Except... they weren't standing anymore. One's shoulder sagged heavily into the car door; head bowed forward so far, his chin nearly touched his chest. The other was bent at the waist, one arm still half-raised toward the pistol at his hip, frozen mid-motion. Both bodies leaned at unnatural angles, as if their strings had been cut, held upright only by the cold metal they had slumped against. Their eyes... hollow voids. Vincent slowed, scanning along the sedan's length.

The driver sat upright, hands on the wheel, head turned slightly toward Vincent's approach. But there was no breath, no blinking or movement, no breathing, just those same empty black sockets where his eyes should have been.

He opened the driver's door. The body spilled out and hit the concrete with a dull thud. Vincent stepped over him and slid into the seat. The leather felt cold, alien beneath his grip. He hadn't driven himself in years and certainly not since he rose high enough that others did it for him.

The door closed. The sound echoed sharply in the empty garage.

He adjusted the rearview mirror out of habit.
And froze. In the reflection, far back where the light faded to shadow, stood Saraphina. Her pale dress faint in the gloom, her crystal blue eyes glimmering like frost in moonlight. She was smiling. Calm. Patient. With cruelty that could not be explained but felt.

His breath caught. "…Saraphina…" he gasped, startled by the sudden vison.

As he blinked.

She was gone.

Only shadows remained. "Fuck me…" he muttered, the words rasping out as the truth sank cold into his bones. His hands shaking on the wheel as he started his vehicle and tried to push down the fear inside him.

Markus hadn't just killed the guards in the conference room; he had erased every man Vincent brought with him. Reminding Vincent just how truly alone he is. A lesson that was made very clear to him now.

The echo of Vincent's engine faded into the distance, swallowed by the night.

Upstairs, the conference chamber was still like a tomb. The bodies of the guards remained exactly where they had fallen, their hollow sockets staring into nothing.

Markus sat at the head of the table, hands resting lightly on the swirling crimson patterns beneath the glass. The smoke-like tendrils inside moved lazily now, as if sated. From near the far windows, the faintest sound of bare feet against marble approached. soft, deliberate steps. Saraphina emerged from the dim, stopping at Markus' side. She tilted her head, looking up at him with crystal blue eyes that reflected the city's lights.

"I hope he comes back?" she asked, her voice almost sing-song, as if discussing a pet that had wandered off. Markus' deep violet gaze lingered on the city skyline. "Only when he's needed."

She smiled. a small, knowing curve of her lips. before drifting away again, her pale dress whispering faintly as she returned to the window. The swirling patterns in the table pulsed once, as though they had heard her, and then settled into stillness.

Chapter 4. A Dinner for Two

The flat was cozy in a way Jessica didn't expect. Not sterile government housing, not some safe house with bare walls and cots, but lived-in: bookshelves sagging with thick leather spines, curtains drawn back to let the city breathe through the balcony doors, and a faint aroma of wine already spilling from the kitchen.

Henry moved easily in the space, like he'd always belonged here. He loosened his tie, set aside his blazer, and busied himself with a pot simmering on the stove. When he glanced back over his shoulder, the faintest of smirks tugged at his lips.

"You look like a woman who's forgotten how to breathe," he said, half-teasing, half-serious.

Jessica dropped into a chair at the table, letting her body sink into the cushion. She hated to admit it, but he was right. Weeks of fluorescent lights, cubicle walls, endless paperwork, her body was still stiff with it. Being pulled into Rome on short notice should've irritated her, but now, sitting here, it felt like oxygen again.

"Don't tell me you cook," she said, eyeing the steam rising from the pan.

Henry raised a brow, gave the pot a deliberate stir, and said nothing. The silence was almost smug.

Jessica chuckled. "I stand corrected."

He brought over two plates, a fettuccine pasta, perfectly tossed, the scent of garlic and cream thick in the air. A bottle of red waited uncorked on the table, its deep ruby catching the lamplight. He poured a glass for her, then took the seat across from her, and raised his glass.

"To Rome," he said.

She clinked her glass to his, savoring the first sip as it rolled warm down her throat. For the first time since landing, she felt her shoulders loosen.

"So," she said, twirling her fork, "what exactly am I doing here? You drag me across an ocean, set me up in a monastery of all places, and tell me it's just routine?"

Henry leaned back, swirling his wine. His expression was calm, practiced after years of this type of case, the kind of calm that told her he'd already rehearsed what to say.

"Routine, yes. But necessary." He tapped his glass against the table. "Some doors are better left shut. That monastery has plenty. Our job or more precisely, your job is just to make sure no one else goes prying where they shouldn't.".

Jessica arched a brow. "That's it? Security babysitting?"

"You say babysitting, I say preservation." His voice softened, carrying a note that might've been pride. "History doesn't need us to rewrite it. It needs us to guard it. Let the monks keep their silence. Let the stones keep their secrets. We're simply making sure of that."

She studied him across the table, her fork poised but forgotten. Henry had always been like this a master at misdirecting conversations and never quite answering directly, always circling the truth like it was something fragile. It was part of what made him such a good historian, she supposed. He catalogued. He observed. He let the record speak while he remained just outside the margins.

"You make it sound noble," she said, finally taking a bite.

He smirked. "Only because it is."

The meal settled into a rhythm. laughter, light teasing, stories from old assignments. Henry spoke of archives and dusty vaults, of "adventures" that Jessica suspected were more paperwork than peril. She offered stories of her own, though most were clipped, polished. the kind of professional summaries she always defaulted to.

But as the wine drained and the night stretched, something inside her began to soften. She wasn't *FBI Special Agent Trainer* right now. She wasn't a case file or a badge. She was just Jessica, across from a mentor who had pulled her out of fluorescent purgatory and dropped her into Rome with a plate of pasta and a glass of red wine that came from the local vineyard just outside the window.

"You've known me too long," she said, shaking her head after he caught her smiling for no reason.

"That's the point," Henry said. "I know when to pull you out of the cave you insist on living in."

She laughed, rolling her eyes, but the truth in his words wasn't lost on her.

For a moment, silence stretched between them, not uncomfortable, but heavy with something unspoken. Henry's gaze lingered on her, not searching, not prying, just…knowing.

Then he raised his glass again, breaking the moment before it could turn into something else. "To the week ahead. Simple, quiet, and routine."

Jessica clinked her glass to his, though a small voice at the back of her mind whispered otherwise.

Chapter 5. Stones That Remember

Rome always looked older from the air.

Jessica had taken a seat calmly in her rideshare on her way back to the site, The morning was early, almost too early, but after dinner, her and Henry would be too excited to sleep, and she almost expected him to already be there. The thought warmed her and brought a smile to her face. She rolled her window down to catch the morning air kissing her face gently. The ride was quiet and calming to her. From the plane Rome did look older, and the rural areas as she had passed over spread and stretched like threading veins through stones that had outlived empires. By the time her rideshare crawled past a barricade and into the monastery perimeter, the sun had lifted just enough to put a stern shine on the old walls.

The place didn't look like a prison was ever part of the foundations at first glance. It looked like a monastery that had put on shackles and learned to endure.

A cluster of vans and a mobile command tent filled the courtyard. Men in blue paper booties and respirators moved coils of ducting-like intestines, feeding them into a grated arch. Someone had painted a quick red X on a door and then circled it twice, angrier the second time.

"Jess!"

Henry's voice cut through the thrum of generators. He strode over in a field jacket, the same grin he always wore when the world got interesting. There were more lines around his eyes than the last time she'd seen him.

"You look terrible," she said, deadpan.

"That's the charm." He gestured toward the main structure. "Welcome to Santa Vetrata. Part prison, part monastery, part... we'll see."

"Any updates on the 'illness'?"

"Symptoms were respiratory and vague. But the crews cleared the wing, and while mapping vents, they found this." He angled his head toward the grating. "Old stone tunnel. Not on any prison plan. The Church sent an attaché to say, politely, that the area beyond might be ecclesiastical. Which is medieval for 'ours.'"

"And the monks?"

"Accommodating, if stern. You'll love it."

They passed under the cloister arcade: arches, shadow, swallows clicking overhead. The air changed when they stepped inside. cooler, denser, with a faint mineral tang. Stone held temperature and secrets the same way.

In the refectory, a thin man in black waited with hands folded. His eyes were kind and iron at the same time.

"Abbot Nicolo," Henry said. "This is Agent Jessica Trainer."

"Welcome," the Abbot said in careful English. "You come to look where we do not."

"We're here to keep everyone safe," Jessica said. "And to understand what we're looking at. With your permission."

"A door was sealed before my grandfather's grandfather's time," the Abbot said. "The ledger records... one word." He glanced to Henry as if seeking permission to say it.

Jessica met his eyes. "What word?"

"Silence."

They walked the cloisters in a hush that felt asked-for rather than enforced. Every few feet, devotional frescoes blinked from the walls: saints with oculi of gold leaf, halos worn thin by humidity and prayer. A novice crossed the far end of the hall, nodded to the Abbot, and vanished into the kind of light that makes dust holy.

Back at the breach, a contractor in a hardhat lifted the grating for them. The tunnel beyond ran cool and low, its stones mortared by hands that had been dust for centuries. Air moved faintly through it. breath the building had saved.

Jessica took the point. Her headlamp picked out fossils of time: old scorch marks, a rusted lantern hook, a length of chain fused to stone. The tunnel narrowed, turned, then ended in a wall of plaster-like bone.

Embedded at shoulder height was a round of iron, half-rotted, half-stubborn: a ring set into the plaster. A seal.

Henry exhaled. "Subtle."

The Abbot arrived behind them with a small wooden box. From it, he drew a simple key. iron, long-shanked, handmade. He held it like he was passing a relic.

"This was kept with the ledger," he said softly.

"Is there... a lock?" Henry asked, squinting at the plaster.

The Abbot shook his head. "The key is ceremonial. The ring opens."

Jessica pulled on nitrile gloves. "Get the scanner in position. I want a live read behind this before we touch it."

A tech rolled the ground-penetrating radar into place, smearing coupling gel on the plaster before sliding the wand in slow arcs. The laptop translated echoes into ghostly strata. Noise. Void. Noise again. Then, softly, a contour of some space beyond. the shape of a chamber. No power signatures. No heat.

"Dead as Roman tax law," the tech muttered.

"Vent masks on," Jessica said. "Abbot, you should step back."

"I will remain," he said. "Faith does not move by distance."

She nodded once. Then she wrapped her fingers around the iron ring.

It was colder than it should have been.

She braced, shifted her weight, and pulled. For a heartbeat, nothing. Then the ring gave a fraction, with a scraping sound like something waking up. Dust whispered down. Cracks splintered and fractured out across the plaster, thin as veins, then thickened into branches. The slab eased, not outward, but inward, as if it had wanted to return to the dark.

A breath of air came through, older than the city above. It smelled of stone, old oil, sealed time.

Henry's voice dropped. "Tell me you feel that."

She did. Not pressure. Not temperature. A… attention. The sense of standing at a threshold that had been waiting specifically for her.

Jessica set her jaw and pulled again. The slab buckled at the seam and tilted inward, then collapsed in a soft, heavy rush. A cloud of powder rolled out around them. For a moment, they all coughed, eyes watering, masks inadequate against centuries.

Her headlamp cut the dark.

A staircase descended into a circular room, the stone smoother than the tunnel, the geometry too precise for a prison, monastic, deliberate, like a prayer made architecture.

She took the first step, Henry at her shoulder, the Abbot two paces back. As her boots touched the chamber floor, her light found carvings in the stone, deep lines and arcs and sigils she recognized from manuscripts but never expected to see with her own eyes. Not apotropaic. Not decorative. Functional.

A chamber made to hold.

The center was empty.

Her lamp moved, skimming the curve of the wall.

The beam swept across a chain sunk into the floor, an iron shackle resting open, its pin set to one side like a sentence interrupted. Nearby, a long, dark stain bled into stone and stayed there.

Henry's voice was very quiet. "Someone wanted whatever was in here to stay in here."

"Or to come back," the Abbot said, almost to himself.

"Let's get full-spectrum imaging," Jessica said, forcing her voice steady. "Lidar, micro. "

She stopped.

Somewhere at the edge of hearing, beneath the generator hum and distant voices above, there was another sound. Not vibration. A cadence. The low drum of something that could have been the building's old heart. Or a pulse. One. Then not-two. Not-human.

Her lamp trembled a fraction. She steadied it. The beam found a second recess in the far curve, half-shadowed, deeper. Something hung there, just at the edge of light: cloth or skin or the idea of a person waiting without breath.

"Jess?" Henry said.

She lifted a hand to quiet him.

Her steps were careful now, her light slow, the circle tightening.

The recess gave back the dark, then a shape, then the suggestion of a face that had been carved by weather and war. The eyes closed. Or not yet open.

Jessica swallowed, the motion loud in her own ears.

"Whatever this was," she murmured, barely more than breath, "it isn't done."

And the stone with years of secrets, the old, obedient stone seemed to agree.

Morning broke with the toll of bells rolling down from the monastery tower, their resonance thrumming through stone like the heartbeat of the place itself. Jessica laced her boots, pulled her braids tight, and stepped into the cold hallways, the air damp with centuries of breath and prayer. The faint smell of baking bread drifted from the kitchens, warm and comforting in contrast to the chill.

Henry was waiting, leaning against a pillar like he belonged there. Two paper cups steamed in his hands, his grin bright in the morning light.

"Coffee?" he asked, offering one out. "Just like you like it."

Jessica arched a brow, skeptical, but accepted. The heat bled into her palms. One sip, and her suspicion faltered. Sweet, smooth, exactly right.

"So, you *can* learn," she said softly.

"Don't sound so surprised," Henry shot back, a smirk tugging at his lips.

She let the warmth linger before replying. "Still recovering from the airport debacle."

He clutched his chest with mock injury. "That was a tactical misstep, not sabotage."

Jessica's laugh carried up into the vaulted ceiling, chasing away the heavy silence of dawn. For a fleeting moment, it was easy.

two colleagues, two friends, falling back into familiar banter. But beneath it all, Jessica felt it: normal never lasted here.

The day unfolded in stone and shadow.

Henry led with his flashlight like a conductor's baton, his enthusiasm spilling over with every step. He narrated crumbling walls, sketched prisoners' stories from graffiti etched into mortar, pointed out ironwork that had somehow resisted rust.

"This wing," he said, sweeping the beam over a row of rotted doors, "held the worst of the worst. Murderers, deserters, thieves. Some of them… never left." His voice dropped on the last words, savoring them.

Jessica smiled faintly, jotting in her notebook. But her eyes wandered. and caught.

A door sealed with iron bands.
Its lock was newer than the wall that held it.

She drifted toward it, curiosity tugging.

"Jess! Over here."

Henry's voice cut through, pulling her back. He stood by a niche in the wall, pointing at deep gouges etched into stone. "See these marks? A prisoner thought he could claw his way to heaven."

It was grotesque, fascinating, and far from the sealed door.

She followed him.

For now.

By midday it had become a pattern.

Not constant.
Not perfect.
But deliberate.

The first time she drifted toward a sealed stairwell, Henry caught up late, breath faintly uneven.

"Sorry. archives snagged me," he said too quickly. "You don't want that wing anyway. It's collapsed."

The second time, when she slowed near a chained iron gate set deep into the masonry, Henry didn't redirect her immediately.

He hesitated.

Just long enough.

Then smiled. "That one's restricted. Old drainage failures."

By the third time. near a corridor bricked with newer stone. he never spoke at all.

He simply stepped into her path.

It wasn't panic.

It was **precision**.

That was when the shape of the day shifted for her. not into suspicion, but into **calculation**. Henry wasn't preventing discovery.

He was managing its **timing**.

That night, Jessica lay in her narrow guest quarters, the stone wall cooled against her back. The wind pressed against the shutters with a low moan, like the monastery itself sighing in its sleep.

She replayed the day. Every detour. Every redirected step. Henry's voice still rang in her ears, earnest and bright. but something about the way he'd steered her sat wrong.

Not fear.

Intention.

Her eyes drifted to the clock.

1:42 a.m.

Perfect.

She slid into her boots, pulled her jacket close, and slipped into the corridor. Her flashlight cut a narrow beam through the dark, every shadow stretching long against the stone.

Tonight, she wouldn't be turned away.
Tonight, she would see what lay behind the doors Henry had never let her reach.

Jessica slipped into the passage like a ghost unremembered by air.

The monastery was a maze after midnight. arches folding into arches, corridors narrowing into veins of stone that seemed to pulse faintly with age. More than once, she found herself facing the same saint twice, the same cracked fresco, the same shadow bent like a familiar spine.

Either she was circling…

Or the building wanted her to.

She tested the doors softly. Most answered with stubborn silence. Some whispered back with dead iron. A few almost too few easily gave beneath her palm only to end in rubble, walls bricked with newer stone, their mortar still pale with recent prayer.

And each time, every time she felt it.

That subtle absence.

Henry wasn't here.

No footsteps redirecting her.
No voice drawing her away.

For the first time since arriving, the monastery had gone quiet in a way that felt **intentional**.

Time lost its shape.

Her watch ticked forward in cold, indifferent increments. **2:03...**
2:41... 3:18...

Fatigue dragged at her limbs. Dust coated her boots. Still, the
pull in her chest only sharpened. The deeper she moved, the
more certain she became that this wasn't curiosity driving her
anymore.

It was **recognition**.

At **4:21**, she found the cloister where the frescoes changed.
At **4:28**, she felt the cold sharpen.
At **4:31**, the air stopped moving.

And at **04:32**, she stood before the steel door the monastery had
tried to forget.

Chapter 7. The Sealed Wing

04:32.

The digits on Jessica's watch glowed a cold, clinical blue. just bright enough to mark how alone she was. The monastery slept behind her: corridors of stone holding their breath, doors breathing out slow drafts of old air, the world reduced to the soft tick of heat in the pipes and the faintest murmur of wind pressing at stained glass.

She moved like a thought no one had spoken aloud.

Her flashlight stayed low, a narrow crescent at her boots. She'd spent hours tracing dead ends, blocking staircases, bricked arches, and iron gates fused with time. Every detour sharpened the same pull in her body, as if the building itself had a pulse and it was drawing her toward it, one careful step at a time.

The wing she'd been steered away from yesterday waited at the far edge of the oldest cloister. Even the frescoes changed here, the saints and martyrs fading into angular figures whose faces had been deliberately scratched away. Dust lay thicker, undisturbed by the traffic of decades. Her breath fogged in the colder air.

The door at the end of the passage wasn't wood at all, as she'd first assumed. It was steel under centuries of paint and smoke, a slab that filled the arch from jamb to jamb. No hinges. No handle. No keyhole. Someone had sealed it from this side and meant it to be final.

Jessica set her light on the floor, the beam knifing across the metal. A seam. Barely. She ran her fingertips along it and found the faintest give. a panel the shape of a palm, flush with the surface. She pressed. Nothing.

She tried again, shifting pressure. Something deep inside the wall answered with a tired click.

Bolts groaned. Invisible pins withdrew with the slow complaint of iron against stone. The slab exhaled a line of powdered soot and edged outward on rails she couldn't see.

Cold air unspooled across her face, sharp and dry as old parchment, mineral and faintly metallic, threaded with the ghost of incense. The smell of a room that hadn't exhaled in centuries.

Jessica picked up the light and stepped through.

The corridor beyond swallowed her. It was narrower and older than the halls above, the masonry noticeably different beneath her beam. larger stones set by a hand that understood permanence. Shelves had been carved directly into the walls and sealed with thick glass panes. Beneath the grime, she could make out rolled scrolls and bound volumes bundled in cord, each labeled in a tidy hand that had gone brown with age.

An occasional jar held things that were not books: a ring of keys fuzzed with verdigris, a sliver of bone, a scrap of cloth with embroidery too fine to be monastic.

Her footsteps softened to nothing on a floor long polished by no one. The tunnel bent once, then flared open without warning into a space so large her light seemed to shrink in her hand.

A library. if the word didn't sound too modern for what this was. Stacks rose from the floor like dark ribs, their upper reaches lost in the rafters. Ladders slept upright against them, wrapped in cobweb lace. The far walls were a collage of alcoves and niches, each cradling reliquaries, iron-bound chests, and small statues whose faces had been worn smooth by centuries of prayer.

And along the right-hand wall, under a run of arched windows bricked up from the outside, lay a row of simple cots.

Eleven of them.

She approached in a slow line, the beam of her light steady even as her pulse was not. The first body had collapsed inward on itself, robe still draped where flesh had once been, hands clasping a wooden crucifix at a chest of dust. Peace lived in the pose. an intentional surrender. The second lay the same. The third.

Eleven monks at perfect rest, as if they had agreed to sleep at the same hour and never wake.

A whisper slid loose in Jessica's throat without meaning to. "What did you keep?"

She kept moving.

The twelfth was not in bed.

He sat at a broad stone desk near the rear of the hall, slumped forward in his chair. The quill had fallen from his hand, dried feather crushed beneath his sleeve. Parchment lay under him, weighted at the corners by smooth river stones. Wax seals crowded the desk's edge, candles guttered to knots of ash, the ink well scraped to the dregs.

Jessica braced both hands on the stone to steady herself. The cold grounded her as the room shifted from discovery into ritual. She raised the light and angled it so the script would catch.

Latin. Neat. Deliberate.
Not a ledger.
Not an inventory.

A journal.

She opened the ancient pages and read.

We have received our charge from the bishop himself, and by his authority we consecrate this wing. We shall not depart it. Our lives seal what stone cannot. The city above will forget what is kept beneath it, and that is mercy.

Her chest rose and fell with each sentence, the words drawing a net around her as tightly as the walls did.

We have taken vows of silence to the outside. To each other we confess our fear. We do not tend a library. we tend a remembrance that must never travel. We were told only this: guard him. Guard him until the end of days. And if our day of judgment should come, do not open at the pleas of men, nor the threats of kings.

The ink grew heavier.

I did not seek him. Providence stumbled me upon a lower hall and a truth older than our order. I do not say it here, for names call power, and the young would read and burn themselves for want of wonder. It is enough that we remain faithful and silent.

The cadence slowed.

We ate our ration with thanksgiving. We prayed in our final hours. We have made this place clean with our last strength. To those who come after, if any: do not look upon your mercy as curiosity. Do not break what we have toiled to hold.

Jessica swallowed. Her eyes slid to the final line.

And **before her mind could fully accept the words, memory struck first.**

Not her memory.

The reader's.

That name.

Already spoken.

Already waiting.

James.

The word did not land as discovery.

It landed as **confirmation.**

Her attention sharpened.

Not *was.*

Is.

His name **is** James… and he **is** eternally damned.

The tense struck her harder than the name.

The room seemed to draw inward around the word. Shelves leaned closer. Dust whispered like breath held too long. This had never been an archive.

It had been a perimeter.

The books were the barrier.
The cots were the cost.

Somewhere in the rafters, a drop of water fell onto stone with a sound far too loud.

Jessica closed her eyes, pulled one breath in, let it out.

When she opened them, the room had not softened.

It never would.

She lifted the quill and set it gently back into its tray as though the monk might wake and reach for it. Her palms left pale crescents in the ancient stone. She stepped back once. Then again.

She had not uncovered a secret.

She had stepped into the continuation of one.

That was when she noticed the shelf.

All the stacks were of the same rough stone. uprights and planks cut directly from the wall itself. All except one near the desk.

Oak.

Thick-planked. Mortised. Pegged.

Out of place the way a single voice is in a choir.

She crossed to it, set her light on the floor again, and ran both hands along the uprights. The wood hummed faintly beneath her touch with the same pressure she'd felt behind the steel door, as if it were holding its breath.

At the base, where stone met wood, something like a seam.

She pressed her shoulder to the shelf and pushed.

Nothing.

She shifted her stance and pushed again.

It moved a fraction, then another, dragging a tired groan from the floor that shuddered through the hall.

She froze. Listened.

Only her heart answered.

"Don't be stupid," she whispered. advice she didn't take.

Behind the shelf, set into the masonry, slept a second door. narrower, older, carved with lines that made her eyes ache if she stared too long. Angels reduced to mathematics. Script reduced to geometry. In its center, not a keyhole but a sunburst of overlapping plates etched in characters she half-recognized from marginalia upstairs. **celestial, not ecclesiastical.**

The pull in her chest quickened to a drumbeat.

A lock was waiting.

To be told a story it would obey.

"Jessica."

Her name, behind her. soft, surprised, too close.

She flinched hard enough that her light skittered a white arc across the ceiling.

Henry stood in the mouth of the tunnel.

"You shouldn't be in here alone," he said, the reprimand buried beneath awe. "My God…"

He stepped past her on instinct, reverent, careful not to disturb the dust. One by one, he paused beside the cots. He didn't touch a thing.

"Have you ever seen anything like this?" she asked softly.

"No," he breathed. "Not in this… condition." He shook his head. "They sealed themselves in."

She nodded. There was nothing else sane to do.

He drifted toward the oak shelf. "Odd… more modern than the rest." His fingers found the worn depression. The shelf shifted. but he stopped it.

"Later," he said gently, with finality. "We do this right."

Jessica's jaw flexed. She let the argument die unspoken.

His name is James… and he is eternally damned.

The word **is** kept ringing.

If the monk had written **is**, then what they guarded was not a relic.

It was a **presence.**

"All right," she said. "Tomorrow."

Together, they slid the oak shelf back into place.

The steel door sealed again like a tomb.

05:11.

Dawn was still only a rumor.

She stood one heartbeat longer than Henry did.

Inside her, the monk's final line continued to echo.

His name is James…

…and if **is** was true.

Then she hadn't discovered a room.

She had stepped to the edge of a living cage.

Chapter 8. The Celestial Key

Henry's voice shattered the stillness, echoing across the chamber like a sudden crack in glass.

"Jessica!"

She froze mid-step, caught near the twelfth monk's stone desk, the parchment still half-lit in her trembling flashlight beam. She turned slowly. Henry's figure filled the threshold, his expression tight. not fury, but the sharp disapproval of a man who felt trust had been betrayed.

"You shouldn't be in here without me." His words were clipped, but his eyes were already moving past her, widening as they fell upon the row of cots.

His voice softened, almost breaking. "…My God."

He stepped inside as though entering a sanctuary. All reprimand forgotten, he drifted from one cot to the next, crouching low to study the skeletal forms. His fingers hovered, reverent but careful, tracing the rotted fabric of robes, the worn beads of rosaries, the crucifixes still clasped in bony hands. Dust spiraled upward at his touch, stirred after centuries of stillness.

Jessica let his awe carry him forward, her own guilt momentarily eclipsed by the sight of him whispering prayers over the monks' remains. She knew Henry well enough to recognize sincerity when she saw it. His reverence was genuine.

But so was her urgency.

She moved quietly, deeper along the far wall, her light sweeping over shelves and cots. The oppressive silence returned, the kind that made her heartbeat feel deafening in her own ears. Every step was calculated, her boots whispering against stone.

Then her beam caught a glimmer.

Beneath the folded hem of a decayed robe, something metallic winked at her. She crouched, hand trembling as she brushed aside the fabric. What she lifted was no crucifix. It was heavier, golden in color, oddly shaped. edges jutting like the teeth of a puzzle. It didn't belong in any monk's possession.

Her breath caught. She slid it into her satchel, the weight thumping against her hip.

She rose, moved to the next cot. Another faint glimmer. This time tucked beneath skeletal fingers. She eased it free, wincing at the dry snap of bone that came with the motion. She froze, heart hammering, half-expecting Henry to look up. But his back was still turned, shoulders bowed in devotion at another bedside.

Jessica slipped the second piece into her satchel.

Two became three. Then four. Each different in its edges, but clearly meant to interlock, to form something greater than themselves. Her fingers brushed over the metal in her bag, the pieces pressing against one another with an almost magnetic draw.

She swallowed hard. Keys. But not to separate doors. No… these were parts of a single whole.

"Jess."

Henry's voice was closer now. She jerked upright, spinning toward him. He was only a few steps away, his eyes still roaming the shelves, his expression solemn. He hadn't noticed her theft. Not yet.

"Look at this," he murmured, brushing his hand along a spidery inscription carved into the wood of a shelf. "It's a record... a cataloging system, maybe. These monks weren't just preserving relics. they were archiving. Documenting. Entire lives reduced to ink and parchment."

Jessica forced herself to step toward him, feigning interest while her satchel weighed heavier with every secret she'd taken.

"Strange, isn't it?" she said softly. "To spend your whole life writing and guarding, only to be buried with the words."

Henry nodded, his gaze fixed on the dust-caked spines before them. "They weren't buried, Jess. They chose this. Locked themselves in, sealed themselves here to die with what they guarded. That's not duty." He glanced at her, eyes shadowed. "That's devotion."

The word lingered in the air, unsettling her more than she let show.

She turned away, her beam falling on a darker shelf tucked into the far corner. Unlike the rest, which were stone, this one was wood. oak, heavy, scarred by centuries. It stood out like a scar among bones.

Something in her chest tightened.

She approached, ran her palm along its surface. The grain felt wrong against her skin, too deliberate, too out of place. She crouched, fingers testing the base. A faint gap. Hollow.

"Henry," she called before she could stop herself.

He was at her side in moments. Together they braced themselves and pushed. The oak shelf scraped against stone, groaning in protest. Dust rained from the ceiling as it shifted inch by inch until at last it slid aside, revealing what had been hidden.

A door.

Smaller than the great steel one that had first barred her path, but far more intricate. Its surface was carved with spiraling sigils, angelic symbols etched in geometric perfection. They intersected like stars in a constellation, their meaning lost but their weight undeniable.

At the center lay a lock. no simple keyhole, but a sunburst of overlapping plates, each etched with script. It looked less like a mechanism and more like a puzzle built to resist any hand unworthy of solving it.

Jessica's breath quickened. Her satchel suddenly felt alive at her side, the puzzle pieces burning against her hip.

But she kept silent.

Henry studied it for a long moment, awe and unease warring on his face. Then he straightened, brushing dust from his hands. "It's late. We'll document this properly in the morning." His tone was final, an attempt to seal away more than just the door.

Jessica bit back on the urge to argue. She forced a smile, nodding once. "Alright. Tomorrow."

But inside, her resolve had already hardened.

Later that Night

The monastery slept, its silence so deep she could hear the faint creak of wood settling in its beams. Jessica lay awake on her cot, the stone walls of her small guest cell closing in around her. The satchel sat at her bedside, heavy with the stolen keys.

Her heart drummed as she sat up. Carefully, she drew the pieces out, laying them one by one across the blanket.

In the pale glow of her flashlight, they gleamed strangely. edges sharp, surfaces etched with designs that caught the light and threw it back in fractured patterns. She turned the first in her hand, sliding it against the second. They resisted at first, then clicked together, not locked but aligned, as if recognizing one another.

Her pulse quickened.

She tried the third. It slotted neatly against the first two, creating a larger arc of metal. The fourth completed the curve, forming not four separate objects, but one of them unlike the others, a single, jagged key with teeth unlike any she had seen before.

She stared at it, the air in her cell suddenly colder, her breath visible in the beam of her light.

A sound broke the silence.

Footsteps. Slow. Passing down the corridor outside her door. The shuffle of sandals against stone. A monk, maybe. But she froze all the same, clutching the assembled key to her chest.

The steps faded. Silence again.

Jessica slid the key apart, tucking the pieces back into her satchel one by one. Her fingers lingered on the last piece, reluctant to let go. The words she had read in the parchment earlier returned to her mind, echoing.

"His name is James… and he is eternally damned."

Not past tense. Present.

Her stomach tightened. That meant whoever this James was… he was still here.

Still waiting.

She lay back; eyes fixed on the dark ceiling above. Sleep never came.

Chapter 9. Covering Tracks

The chill in the monastery's lower halls was the kind that seeped into bones, a cold that felt older than memory. Jessica adjusted her satchel as she followed Henry deeper into the Sanctuary Wing. The air was incense and old stone layered over something sharper, metallic, faint but ever-present here.

The vaulted corridor ahead was lined with faded tapestries. battles, saints, winged figures, their colors leeched by time until they were more ghosts than cloth. Her eyes swept over the walls, searching for any disruption in the rhythm of age.

At the far end, half-shrouded in shadow, a steel-banded door loomed. Corroded hinges. Engravings she didn't quite recognize. A quiet, electric awareness skittered across her chest at the sight.

Henry slowed but did not stop. "We'll take the long route," he said lightly, already turning down a side passage.

Jessica cast one last look at the door before following. Her pulse noted it. Her mind mapped it.

Late Night Resolve

Hours later, the wind hissed along the eaves of her quarters, bringing the smell of rain. Her desk was a chaos of sketches and notes, all circling back to the sealed wing. Henry's "detours" weren't coincidence they couldn't be she thought for a moment they were precise. He was keeping her away.

She flipped to a blank page and wrote in block letters: **THREE DAYS. Map the wing. Speak to the elders. Gather clues. Door last.**

Three days to prepare so well that nothing could stop her.

Day One: The Long Game

Rain slicked the stones by morning, the cloisters echoing with the steady drip of water into deep drains. Jessica walked beside Henry, responding politely to his endless notes on repairs and records while mentally marking every hallway.

She slipped away midmorning on the pretense of checking for water damage in the archives. Brother Ansel found her instead, sipping tea in a shadowed corner.

"You've been asking about the ones who came before," he said, no accusation in his tone.

"They interest me," Jessica replied.

"They kept apart. Always working. Always watching... not *what*. Who."

A warning glimmered in his eyes before he left her alone.

Day Two: The Key

Henry buried himself in cataloging relics. Jessica translated inscriptions, her fingers brushing dust from an old velvet-lined case. and touching cold brass. A small, oddly cut key.

Henry's gaze flicked toward it. "Nothing important," he said.

She slipped it into her pocket anyway.

Day Three: The Plan

The monastery was hushed in the hours after evening prayer, its long stone corridors holding the silence like a chalice. Candles guttered low in their sconces, casting walls in wavering gold and shadow. Jessica moved through it like a shadow of her own, her boots whispering against ancient flagstones.

She carried no lanterns. She didn't need one. Every twist of the halls had become familiar these last days. the rhythm of patrols, the turns that led to the cloisters, the doors that stayed locked at night. She had mapped it all in her mind, piece by piece, waiting for this night.

The first stop was the kitchen. Its heavy oak door creaked slightly, but she slipped through with the ease of a thief.

An old monk sat at one of the tables, his head bowed over a clay cup. The sharp, pungent scent of brandy clung to the air. His snores rolled softly, punctuated by the occasional drunken murmur. Jessica paused, her heart stilling. But he didn't stir.

Her eyes found what she needed.

The pantry was lined with jars and bottles, dry goods and oils stacked high. She gathered what would burn hottest, then crouched to mix it with quiet, deliberate movements. A makeshift accelerant, crude but effective. Nearby, a stub of candle would serve as her timer, its flame slowly eating wax toward the fuel.

She straightened, tucking the candle into place, balancing the small contraption as carefully as a puzzle box.

Her lips curved in a humorless whisper.
"Oh, the things I could do if I were a criminal."

She glanced back at the monk. Still asleep. Still drunk.

"Hopefully this isn't too big of a mess later," she muttered. "Four, maybe five hours… hopefully."

With that, she slipped back into the corridor, leaving the faint smell of spirits and wax behind her.

The monastery was quiet again, the silence broken only by her steady breath. She adjusted her grip on the key, its warmth steady in her palm. It was almost like it wanted her to keep going, to finish what she had started.

The north wing loomed ahead.

A towering bookcase blocked the sealed door as though the monks themselves feared what lay behind it. Jessica braced her shoulder against the weight and pushed. The wood groaned across the floor, her muscles trembling with the effort until the doorway yawned wide before her.

The blackened steel of the hidden door gleamed faintly in the half-light; its surface etched with intricate angelic carvings that pulsed with a faint inner glow.

Jessica let out a slow breath, her chest tight. She pressed the key into the lock. It didn't fit.

Instead, a panel slid open with a metallic click. Inside waited a mechanism older than the monastery itself, its gears and plates tarnished but intact. Her hand went to the sketches she had painstakingly drawn. the pieces fit exactly.

Her pulse surged as she twisted the key.

Bolts shifted. Metal groaned. Dust sifted from the ceiling.

And then the door exhaled. a rush of air stale with centuries, breathing out into the corridor.

Jessica stood very still, the key warm in her hand, the massive door before her alive with whispered promise.

She stepped into the dark.

Chapter 10. Beyond the Sealed Door

The lock gave way with a groan that seemed older than the stones themselves. Dust spilled like breath as the massive door yawned inward, exhaling air that had not tasted freedom in centuries.

Jessica's flashlight cut a narrow cone into the dark. The beam barely pushed against the black, swallowed whole within a few feet, the shadows shifting as if alive. The air inside pressed against her chest. damp, metallic, and heavy with something more than age. It was as though memory itself had weight here.

Symbols traced along the stone walls, half-erased by centuries of neglect. The mortar lines bent unnaturally, deliberate curves forming runes that prickled beneath her skin. The hum she had felt from the door earlier throbbed here in her bones, steady as a buried drumbeat.

The corridor narrowed, forcing her shoulders to scrape against the walls. Stone dust clung to her coat as she squeezed through until suddenly the passage opened, spilling her into a vast antechamber. Collapsed columns leaned drunkenly against the walls, broken statues stared with gouged-out eyes, and carved figures twisted across the stone. Their faces had been defaced long ago, but their sharp outlines still conveyed menace.

Her boots crunched on fragments scattered across the floor. At first, she thought of them as small stones, but the hollow crack under her step revealed a brittle bone, fused so completely with rubble she could not tell one from the other.

The ground grew slick beneath her. Jessica crouched, hand braced against the floor, her flashlight tumbling from her grip. As she reached for it, she froze.

Her eyes widened. For a moment, she thought her mind had betrayed her. A shape loomed against the far wall. a man.

He was suspended by chains thick as her wrists, drawn in every direction, pulling his body into a grotesque cruciform tension. His toes barely brushed the stone, straining against the pull. His form had withered, gaunt to the point of breaking. Skin stretched over sharp bones; muscles atrophied until he looked like a relic. a husk of life kept just shy of death.

Her breath caught. The helmet that encased his head was unlike anything she had ever seen: a cage of iron and gold, etched with symbols that glowed faintly even in this darkness. It sagged with such weight that his spine arched, vertebrae protruding sharply beneath skin that seemed too thin to hold them. From beneath its rim spilled a long, tangled beard, white and coarse, cascading over his chest.

The first thought that came was prison. Whoever he was, this was no burial it was much deeper, it was confinement.

Jessica crept closer, each step ringing against the chains. She stared at the figure, pity twisting in her chest. His frailty screamed of suffering; his body so close to collapse that she almost prayed he had already died.

A whisper escaped her lips before she could stop it.
"I'm sorry… dear God, I'm so sorry…"

The head jerked.

The chains clattered violently as the body spasmed. Jessica stumbled back, her heart launching into her throat. Her soul felt as though it had leapt from her body entirely. She screamed, her voice echoing across the chamber:

"Christ! He's alive!"

The man dragged air into his lungs. heavy, rattling gasps that filled the chamber. Then his skin began to glow. Faint lines etched across his body, tattoos unseen until they blazed to life. The light grew brighter, searing, until steam hissed off his flesh.

Flame burst from him. White fire engulfed his body, the chains ringing under the heat. He screamed into the mask. a guttural, muffled cry that rattled stone dust from the ceiling. Jessica shielded her eyes, the heat blasting against her skin as the impossible transformation burned before her.

And then it ended.

The fire collapsed inward, leaving only the smoldering remains of a charred husk hanging in the chains. Smoke curled upward, acrid and metallic. Beneath the blackened flesh, faint lines of light still pulsed. the tattoos glowing softly like embers refusing to die.

Jessica stared in horror.
"What the hell was that…?" she whispered. "He has to be dead…"

She forced herself closer, step by step, searching for the trap, the mechanism, anything that might explain what she'd seen. Her eyes fell on the chains. Every link shimmered faintly, carved with angelic script, glyphs that twisted and glowed with something not of this world.

Her hand reached out, trembling. As her fingers brushed the metal, light surged. The runes blazed white-hot, and the chains dissolved into molten vapor that sank into the stone like water poured on sand.

The charred crusted body dropped, slamming against the floor. The helmet rang with a sharp metallic crack.

Jessica flinched but forced herself to kneel. Her breath quickened as she looked. The charred husk breaking away from the impact of the ground. The skin peeled away in flakes of ash, revealing flesh beneath it. The skin smooth, unburnt, unscarred. Muscle rippled under perfect skin. A transformation was taking place before her eyes, the charred ruin sloughing away to reveal a body reborn.

Her gaze drifted to the helmet.
"Might as well," she whispered, steeling herself.

Her fingers slid beneath the jaw, and with surprising ease the helmet slipped free.

It revealed not a monster. Not a corpse.

But a man.

His face was young, impossibly beautiful, sculpted and strong as if marble had been carved to breathe. A smooth shaved head reflected in the dimness of her light. His lips parted, and his chest rose faintly.

For a heartbeat, his eyes flickered open. A shimmer of amber irises filled with a smoldering molten, unearthly, glowing from within.

Jessica gasped. He exhaled, and then his eyes rolled closed, plunging back into the abyss of unconsciousness.

Her breath trembled. She could only stare.

From the corridor behind came a voice.
"Jess?" Are you in here?" Henry's voice, closer than she wanted.

Another voice interrupted sharply. "Brother Henry. the kitchen! There's a fire!"

Jessica's chest tightened with guilt. She knew. That fire was her doing.

She froze in the darkness, listening as the footsteps retreated. Voices faded into the distance. She was alone again, the unconscious man at her feet.

And in the suffocating silence of the chamber, the weight of what she had done pressed down on her.

Chapter 11. The Prisoner

The monastery had a way of swallowing sound, as if the stone itself remembered vows and kept them. Even so, Jessica waited a full minute after the last set of footsteps faded before she moved. The assembled key lay warm in her palm, its interlocking teeth catching the flashlight beam like a star made of blades.

0445, If she was going to do this, it had to be now.

She slipped into the hall, ghosted past cold niches and rusted sconces, and followed the route she had memorized in the dark: down the infirmary ramp, past the collapsed stairwell, right at the cracked fresco of Saint Bartholomew. The sealed wing breathed a different air. denser, colder, with a tang of iron that coated the tongue. The kind of air that made lungs sting and prayers feel very far away.

At the end of the corridor the oak bookcase loomed like a sentry. She braced and slid it aside. The stone groaned as dust lifted in pale tendrils, and there it was: the inner door, its surface carved with spiraling sigils that seemed to shift if she didn't look straight at them. In the center, the sunburst lock. overlapping plates etched with script that recoiled from the light.

Her fingers trembled as she presented the key. The pieces she'd stolen from the dead fit together with a surety that felt almost biological, as though they missed one another and were relieved to be whole. She aligned the teeth with the plates and pressed.

Nothing moved. The door remained perfectly, arrogantly still.

Jessica exhaled, reset her grip, and turned the key a hair's breadth.

Every etched plate rotated in sympathy. the patterns slid into new constellations, lines aligning until the sunburst resolved into a single sigil. Beneath her palm, something answered. A deep click, like a bone setting. The lock inhaled.

Bolts in the wall withdrew one after another, a chain of heavy sighs passing along the stone. Dust shook from the lintel in a slow, gray rain. The door exhaled a breath of air that had not touched a lung in centuries. It smelled of vellum and extinguished candles. and beneath that, the metallic hush of old blood.

She pushed.

Darkness opened its mouth.

The first steps were careful, heel to toe, the beam of her light narrow and tight. The tunnel beyond was colder than the wing. the kind of cold that climbed bones rather than skin. Each breath fogged in the cone of her flashlight. The walls were lined with stone shelves, glass jars nested like sleeping eyes. Inside them: curls of parchment, cracked ink, ribbons of scripts in a dozen hands. Dust lay on everything like frost.

The tunnel widened into the chamber, and the chamber made her stop.

A library had been carved out of the earth. not only shelves but ladders, desks, cots. Pages pinned under river stones. Ink thrones. An entire life of writing sunk beneath a monastery and forgotten. Far along the wall lay the line of beds, eleven shapes grown thin with time, their robes collapsed, their rosaries like constellations scattered against bone. The twelfth sat upright at a desk, quill fallen from skeletal fingers, head bowed as if in prayer over a page.

She edged closer, the light skating across the parchment. The Latin was meticulous despite the tremor frozen in the strokes. She could read enough.

A charge was given us by the bishop to guard what the Church would not name. We sealed ourselves in obedience. We did not seek him; we found him by accident, and by the mercy of our ignorance we did not flee. He spoke little, but I wrote often. This is our last vigil, and I am the last to keep it. His name is James... and he is eternally damned.

Not *was*. *Is*.

Her breath fogged the edge of the page. The words rippled through her like cold water. If *is*, then this was not only a tomb.

It was a prison.

The pull that had gnawed at her since the first door was stronger now. not sound, not thought, but a weight, a pressure on the sternum. It drew her eye to the far side of the chamber, where the shelves thinned to a blacker dark. She lifted the beam and found, at the limit of light, an archway swallowed in shadow.

"I shouldn't," she whispered, and stepped through anyway.

The arch opened onto a nave of stone. a cathedral buried beneath a monastery. A single aisle of granite led to a dais, and on the dais, hung from the ceiling by chains as thick as her wrists, was a man.

At first he didn't read as a man. He read as architecture. lines and angles and the geometry of restraint: wrists pulled to opposing rings, ankles parted, spine drawn long by the weight at his crown. Then the beam found skin, and the truth assembled itself all at once in her mind.

He was impossibly thin, each rib a stave under bruised parchment, each tendon pronounced as wire. His feet just brushed the stone, enough to relieve nothing. Across his chest and shoulders, tattoos in a language that looked older than writing webbed like constellations: arcs and sigils, whorls and notations that glowed faintly as if tin had learned to remember light.

His head was caged in steel.

The helmet swallowed everything from brow to nape. a smooth, featureless helm engraved in tight lattices of angelic script. Only his jaw showed: a stubborn angle, the pale stubble like frost against marble skin. The weight of the metal dragged his neck until the vertebrae bunched like knuckles beneath the skin.

The chains that crucified him were etched, too, each link scored with the same luminous script. They pulsed with the faintest gold, a heartbeat at the limit of sight.

Her first thought was not horror. It was pity. He looked so fragile that if she cut him down he would shatter.

Jessica's hand rose before she told it to. She placed her fingertips against the nearest chain.

Heat bloomed under her skin.

White-gold flared from the etchings and raced along the length of the shackle like lightning caught in wire. Each link illuminated as it passed, the glow darting into seams and rivets, seeking. The metal vibrated under her hand with a note that thrummed in bone.

She snatched her fingers back on instinct.

The chain went liquid.

It didn't melt and run; it unmade itself. The lines of script burned to ash-bright, then the iron softened, sagged like wax, and thinned to steam that drifted downward and vanished into the stone as though the floor were drinking it. The cuff opened with a sigh. His left arm dropped an inch, and the entire geometry of him changed. a new angle born, a new ache released.

Her heart climbed into her throat. She reached for the next chain.

The moment her skin touched the etched letters, the light recognized her. It leapt to greet her touch. raced the length. unmade the iron.

Another inch. Another.

When the last wrist-cuff opened, his body sagged forward, caught only by the weight at his head. The helmet chain tautened; the script along its plates flashed once, warning or welcome she couldn't tell.

"I'm sorry," she whispered so quietly it echoes in the chamber and her heart meant it. "Dear God, I'm sorry."

The helm answered.

A note rose out of it. not sound, exactly, but pressure. and then the engraved plates along the crown brightened from ember to coal to a white that had color inside it. The air above the dais pinched and warped, the way heat over a road will blur a car to a phantom. Jessica took one step back, then another, and then there was no more room to move.

He inhaled.

It sounded like stone drowning.

His chest expanded against old straps, the skin along his ribs glowing beneath the tattoos, and then a blaze roared outward from under his skin as if he had been lit from within by a match the size of a sun. White fire bled through pre-existing lines, following the map of his markings etched deep into his skin and then abandoned the map entirely and took him.

He screamed.

The helmet swallowed the sound, turned it metallic, muffled and far away, but she could feel it in her own throat, the way a thunderclap can vibrate your sternum. Heat rolled off him in waves that slapped her face and singed the fine hairs along her wrist. She threw an arm up, squinting into her own light. The air stank of nothing she knew, it wasn't the stench of burned hair, not flesh; a pure, hot scent like a kiln opening after centuries.

The fire did not spread. It bloomed through him alone, a contained sunrise. Skin blackened and split with a sound like paper tearing roughly then cracked in polygonal plates that curled at the edges and lifted. Beneath the ruin, new skin lay unblistered and impossible, as if marble had learned to breathe.

She pressed herself to the nearest column to keep from stepping into that light. The glow climbed into the helmet, rattled the plates, and the engraved script along its surface screamed. not in sound, but in meaning. and flickered.

Then the blaze began to die.

The chamber darkened by increments, the way a storm calms. The air stuttered with cooling. Steam rose off his shoulders in lazy, ribboned ghosts and hung under the arch. Char flaked from him in sheets, slipped from deltoids and hips and thudded wetly to the stone. The shackles at his ankles, last to relent, gave up with two soft clicks. His toes kissed the dais cleanly for the first time in. how long? A century? More?

The helmet tipped and settled heavy. He sagged.

Jessica lowered her arm. Her flashlight stuttered from the heat, then steadied. She stared.

Where ruin had been, beauty remained, and the instant left her almost angry. No one should look like that. The planes of his torso had the precise geometry of something chiseled rather than grown; each muscle resolved with a certainty that felt unfair. Veins mapped themselves like watered ink along his forearms. The tattoos that marked his skin in patterns of those constellations buried deep into the night skies had dimmed to a bare whisper again, only occasionally pricking like distant stars.

He was younger than the bones had promised. Early thirties, if that. The stubble at his jaw was pale and soft, new as frost. His mouth was severe. His breathing was steady, sticky with steam.

She touched the helmet.

Even through her glove she felt the script bite. The plates were not only engraved; they were written upon. a palimpsest of angelic language worked so deep the metal had learned to remember it. She curled her fingers under the edge at his jaw, and the weight told its secret: it was *meant* to be removed, but only by a hand it would permit.

"Please," she said, absurdly. To iron. To fate. To him.

She lifted. The seal broke with a dry kiss. The helmet slid in her hands, unexpectedly obedient, and when she pulled it free the web of script guttered and went dark.

It almost fell from her fingers; she barely caught it before the crown hit the dais. She lowered it to the stone and only then looked up.

His face was all at once.

It had the cold logic of a sculpture and the unwanted warmth of a man. High cheekbones, a straight nose that had been broken once and healed perfectly, lips that had learned to close against too much speaking, lashes pale as ash. Even streaked with soot and sweat, even slack with exhaustion, he was the most beautiful thing she had ever seen. Not pretty. Beautiful in a way that had gravity.

His eyes opened.

They were not human in those first seconds they opened into the world again, not because of color (amber, light caught in honey), but because she had the stupid, absolute certainty that they were old enough to remember when light was invented. They flicked across her face and fastened on her mouth, her eyes, her mouth again trying to focus but unable to decide what she was.

"James," she inhaled sharply, not because she had decided to say it but because the name found a mouth.

Something like recognition, or pain, or both, crossed his eyes. They fluttered, and he fell backward into the kind of unconscious that has no dreams.

Only then did she realize she was crying. She wiped at her face with a furious hand and failed to get herself under control. The room felt both too big and too close, the air was too thin, the light too loud.

Footsteps echoed in the library beyond.

She froze, light snapping off by reflex. The darkness pressed against her eyelids like velvet.

"Jess?" Henry's deep voice resonated and echoed down the chamber, it sounded too nearby. The sound softened by distance but unmistakable. "Jessica are you here?"

She swallowed. Her tongue stuck to the roof of her mouth. She did not answer.

Other voices layered in. monks, clustered and disgruntled: "Brother Henry the kitchen, the fuse box" "Smoke!! it's the old oven," "Hurry, please!"

Guilt stabbed through her belly so cleanly she almost laughed. Her own fuse. Her own candle. Her own hour bought with a fire that now bit at the monastery above.

"Coming," Henry called back to them, urgency in his tone. She could hear his footsteps shifted, the sound receded, henry turned back. "Jessica, where have you gone? His voice faded into the tunnels. The door thumped closed. Silence returned like a held breath finally released.

She switched the light on again. The world obeyed.

"Okay," she whispered to the man who had just been on fire. "Okay."

He was impossibly heavy when she got her arm under his shoulders, not the dead weight of sleep but the density of something that shouldn't be carried by a single person. It felt like moving a statue that had decided to breathe. Her knees nearly buckled on the first pull, and she understood in a dull, immediate way that she was about to do something her body would hate her for.

"Step one," she muttered, teeth grit. "Don't get caught with a mysterious naked man."

The ridiculousness of the situation saved her from panic. She looped his arm around her neck, braced her legs, and hauled. His heel scraped the dais, then the aisle, the sound of it loud enough to make her flinch each time. She paused at the arch to listen. nothing but the slow drip of somewhere, and the distant cough of the monastery alive with a controlled emergency.

She dragged him into the library's shadow and laid him gently among the dust. Steam still lifted from his skin in small, ghostly sighs. She found one of the linen blankets folded near the cots, shook gray webs into the air, and returned. The weave caught on the ridges of his shoulders as she spread it across him, tugging it high to his collarbone, lower to his hips.

Her light caught for an instant on the helmet where it lay. Script dead. Steel quiet.

She thought of the line in Adam's hand.

His name is James… and he is eternally damned.

Her hand, without asking her permission, found his cheek. The heat had faded to something human, the kind that lives in a body and means life. His stubble rasped softly against her fingertips.

"Not tonight," she whispered to the room that used to be a tomb. "Not on my watch."

Somewhere above, a bell rang. fast and bright. and was answered by feet running in corridors.

Jessica slid her arms beneath him again and began the long, impossible work of getting him home.

Chapter 12. The Escape

Dead Weight in Holy Halls

He was heavy in a way that defied all reason. not just the weight of flesh and bone, but the crushing density of stone given breath. Dragging him was like trying to move a monument, and Jessica quickly realized she hadn't grasped the impossibility of the task until her arms were already locked under his shoulders.

The moment his full weight sagged into her; her knees nearly collapsed. His body pressed into her chest like a slab of granite, unyielding and merciless, every strained step forcing her lungs to fight for air. The stone floor beneath her boots gave no forgiveness it was slick in places with condensation, jagged in others where centuries had split the mortar.

By twenty steps her arms trembled, her biceps screaming as if threads were tearing loose. By forty, her thighs shook violently, sweat blinding her eyes, and the copper tang of blood filled her mouth where she had bitten her cheek to stay silent.

The monastery's labyrinth unfolded like an unending punishment. Corridors stretched on with cruel indifference, each bend revealing yet another row of torchlit tapestries. Saints, martyrs, and cardinals gazed down from their woven thrones, their threadbare faces stiff with silent condemnation. Shadows stretched and snapped across the walls as flames guttered, every flicker painting her crime in strokes of gold and black.

"Yeah, yeah," she muttered between clenched teeth, dragging him another step forward. "Sinning in the holiest halls. You'll just have to forgive me."

Her satchel strap dug into her shoulder like a brand; its weight now trivial compared to the man she hauled. He didn't stir. Not a twitch. Not a breath loud enough to hear above her own ragged gasps. The pale shimmer of his skin beneath the remnants of soot seemed almost luminous, the sculpted lines of his body catching the torchlight like carved marble.

His hair, damp with sweat and steam, spilled over her arm in loose strands the color of white gold, catching sparks of firelight with each stumble. His face. regal, impossibly symmetrical. bore the peaceful stillness of a sleeping prince carved for a tomb. Except she had seen this man burn alive, had smelled his flesh char and fall away. And yet here he was, whole, untouched, a myth in her arms.

Every corridor was a gauntlet, every corner another chance for discovery. The scrape of his heels echoed against the stones like a drumbeat of guilt. Her pulse leapt with every sound. the whisper of sandals on stone, the distant murmur of monks reciting prayers, the hollow toll of bells bleeding through the walls. At any moment, she expected light to flare around the corner, a monk's candle to reveal her dragging a naked, impossibly beautiful stranger through consecrated halls.

Her heart wouldn't slow. Her body wouldn't stop. Inch by inch, she pressed forward, haunted by both the weight she carried and the truth she couldn't shake she had freed something the monastery had gone to extraordinary lengths to keep buried.

At last, the yawning arch of the main library chamber appeared ahead, a reprieve from the endless corridors. She staggered inside and collapsed beside him, lowering his body to the stone floor with a grunt that broke into a sob.

The braziers glowed steadily in here, painting him in warm light. He looked even less human now, the golden shimmer beneath his skin faint but constant, the soot falling away to reveal smooth, flawless flesh. He was terrible and magnificent all at once.

Jessica touched his cheek again, fingers brushing away a streak of soot, the stubble at his chin rasping softly against her skin. Something inside her ached, sharp and disorienting, a pull she didn't understand. She shivered and forced herself to stand.

The library was too open. Too dangerous. She needed shadow. She needed to disappear.

And then she saw it. a linen closet tucked into a side alcove; its wooden door cracked just enough to promise darkness.

Her arms screamed in protest as she bent down again. The next trial began.

A Cellar to Breathe In

The narrow arch forced her to stop as she dragged him inside. The door gave a long, traitorous groan before shutting, plunging them into the suffocating dark of the cellar.

The air was thick, stale with the scent of cold dust and rotting wood. Shelves leaned drunkenly beneath the weight of forgotten linens, cracked jars, and moth-eaten cloth. Shadows gathered like conspirators, broken only by the shaky circle of her flashlight.

She lowered him at last, gracelessly, his body striking the packed earth with a dull thud that reverberated through her bones. Jessica slumped back against the wall, chest heaving, the sweat on her skin chilled instantly by the damp air. Every breath scalded her lungs. Her arms trembled as though they were no longer her own.

"Step one: don't get caught with a mysterious naked man," she whispered hoarsely, dragging her palms down her face. "Step two…" Her eyes darted over the shelves. Dust. Jars. Cloth. Nothing useful. "…Nope. There is no step two."

Silence pressed close, alive in its own way. Every drip of condensation echoed too loud. Every scratch of mice hidden in the walls set her teeth on edge.

And then there was him, unconscious and breathing steadily.

He lay utterly still, steam still curling from his body in slow waves. The faint golden glow beneath his skin pulsed like a hidden heartbeat, spilling light along the carved ridges of his muscle. He looked impossibly sculpted, almost too flawless, too deliberate, as if he had been designed rather than born.

The smell drifted toward her again. Not burnt flesh, but something wild, unearthly, a musk like cedar smoke after a storm, laced with sweetness that clung to the back of her throat. It filled her chest and unraveled her focus, making her lightheaded.

Jessica knelt beside him before she realized it, fingertips brushing a streak of soot from his jawline. The soft rasp of stubble against her skin made her chest tighten in ways she wasn't ready to name. He was beautiful. Unfairly so. The kind of beautiful that unsettled, that whispered of danger wrapped in allure.

Her hand lingered longer than it should have. She drew it back sharply, pressing her spine to the cold stone wall, arms wrapped tight around her knees.

"Alright, mystery man," she whispered into the thick dark, "if these muscles are magic, I'm billing whatever ancient gym you crawled out of."

The joke died in the air, swallowed by shadows. She let her head tip back against the wall, staring at the low beams above. Just a few minutes, she told herself. Just enough to breathe. Then she'd move him again.

But even as she thought it, she knew the truth: time was slipping through her fingers, and the longer she stayed here, the less control she had.

The Longest Walk of Her Life

They moved in brutal bursts. drag, brace, breathe. Every pull threatened to tear her arms from their sockets, every lurch another battle in a war she couldn't win.

The monastery's rhythm became her lifeline. Bells echoed faintly through the stone, a hollow measure of time. She counted heartbeats between them, using the silence to dart from one shadow to the next. The scuff of sandals, the low hum of prayers, the clink of dishes in distant kitchens. all became signposts, warnings of when to stop, when to move.

Twice she pressed flat behind massive tapestries, lungs burning as shadows swept past the floor beneath her. The dust clogged her throat, threatened to make her cough. She bit the inside of her cheek until blood filled her mouth again, praying the pounding of her heart wasn't loud enough to give her away.

Another time she froze behind a carved pillar as a lone monk passed with a candle. The flame swayed perilously close, its light crawling across the wall until it nearly kissed her face. Her lungs screamed for air, but she didn't breathe, not until the monk's sandals whispered into silence down the corridor.

Every step past that was agony. Her shoulders throbbed like they were tearing loose. Her forearms were numb, her knuckles raw. Her spine burned like a single taut wire.

"You're lucky I like a challenge," she muttered under her breath, dragging him forward another agonizing stretch. "Because leg day is officially canceled for my next lifetime."

The saints above glared at her from the tapestries. men and women of faith stitched in reverence; their eyes flat with judgment. Add it to the list, she thought bitterly, teeth gritted. Just add it to the list.

Her legs buckled more than once. She leaned into the wall, whispering to herself, "Just a little further. Just don't get caught."

But her eyes betrayed her resolve. Every time her flashlight skimmed across his face flawlessly, sculpted, the dim faint light still flickering beneath his skin. Her chest tightened. It wasn't just his weight she was dragging. It was the impossible burden of who he was. And what she had set free.

Sanctuary in Sight

The hallway felt endless.

Jessica's breath came ragged, each step a battle against the burn in her legs. The weight she dragged with her seemed impossible for one person to bear, and yet she clung to it, hauling him one desperate step at a time. Her palms stung, her shoulders screamed, but she didn't stop. not when the chamber door loomed at the far end like salvation itself.

Her knees nearly buckled as she fumbled with the latch. The iron handle slipped twice beneath her sweat-slicked fingers before she forced it down and shoved with her shoulder. The hinges shrieked like something alive, the sound cutting through the silence of the hall. She didn't care. With a final grunt and slow burning heave, she hauled him across the threshold, kicking the door shut with her heel.

The bed groaned under the weight of him as she muscled his body onto the mattress. The frame dipped violently, protesting beneath the unnatural heft of his form. Steam still drifted in faint curls from his skin, rising into the chill of the room, his chest rising and falling in maddening calm. as though he hadn't just been pulled from centuries of torment.

Jessica stood doubled over, palms braced to her knees, her lungs searing with each pull of air. The wool throw at the edge of her bed caught her eye. She grabbed it and draped it across him. It barely reached from chest to hips, a pitiful covering against his presence, but it was all she had to give.

Her gaze stayed on him, unblinking. The shimmer beneath his skin pulsed faintly, a quiet glow fighting to remain hidden, and she felt her stomach tighten. He looked impossibly still. Impossibly perfect. Too much for the human eye to hold without wanting to look away.

Jessica sank into the nearest chair. The wood creaked under her weight as she collapsed, pressing her palms to her face. Stars burst behind her eyes, a wash of white against the dark. Her mind spun, a cyclone of thoughts: the sealed chamber, the monks, Adam's words.

You did it.

The voice wasn't hers she sounded different now, it couldn't be but never the less it rang through her all the same.

She dragged her hands down, smearing the sweat across her cheeks, forcing her trembling into stillness. She tied her hair back with quick, sharp motions, as though braids could anchor her sanity.

"You did it," she whispered hoarsely. Her eyes flicked back to him, lying motionless, a specter wrapped in borrowed wool. "You absolute lunatic. You actually did it."

The chair felt like it might swallow her whole. The longer she sat, the smaller she felt. The silence pressed too heavily, too accusingly, until she couldn't stand it anymore. With effort that scraped against her bones, she forced herself upright.

Her boots whispered across the stone as she crossed the chamber to the door. She slid the bolt into place with a sharp *click*. The sound echoed like judgment, louder than it should, sealing the outside world away.

Jessica let her back fall against the wood, her head tilting back, eyes fluttering shut. For a single heartbeat, she allowed herself to rest there, breathing in the smell of the room: old stone, faint smoke from the fireplace, and the strange ozone tang still clinging to him.

For the first time since she touched those glowing chains, the world outside felt impossibly far away.

"I'm not crazy," she whispered. Her voice cracked. "I didn't just drag a man from some ancient crypt into my bed. I'm not crazy…"

The words trembled in the air, brittle, ready to break.

Her gaze drifted back to him. Steam still curled faintly from his frame, his chest rising with each impossibly calm breath. His jaw was exposed, sharp beneath the faint white stubble, and she found herself staring at the human softness of it. at odds with the impossible weight of his presence.

A shudder worked through her chest. She wasn't sure if it was fear, awe, or something worse.

Her lips parted, a question forming without sound. Who are you?

The silence swallowed the question before it left her mouth.

Jessica moved toward the window, pulling the heavy curtains closed until the neon glow of Rome was smothered. She turned down the lamp until the chamber swam in near darkness. Her every motion was careful, ritualistic, as if any sound might wake him, or summon the world outside to her door.

For a moment, she allowed herself the illusion of sanctuary.

Then the knock came.

Solid. Loud. Final.

Jessica froze. Every drop of blood in her body turned to ice.

"...Jessica?"

Henry's voice.

Her chest clenched so hard it hurt.

The wool throw was askew across him. She darted forward, tugging it higher to cover as much of his body as she could. The shimmer beneath his skin was still faintly visible, but maybe, just maybe, it would pass for shadow under dim light.

Another knock. Harder this time.

"Jessica?"

Her heart slammed once, twice, against her ribs. She stood rigid in the dark, every breath shallow, the walls pressing in. The chamber, which had felt like sanctuary only moments ago, now felt too small, too fragile, ready to shatter at the first wrong word.

Chapter 13. The Name that Burns

The Knock

Two polite raps against the door. "Jessica?" Henry's voice. calm, casual, far too close. "It's early for you. Thought you might want breakfast."

Jessica smoothed her hair with shaking fingers, buying seconds, and cracked the door. Henry stood there holding a small paper-wrapped bundle of fruit, wearing that warm, practiced smile she'd seen charm donors, dignitaries, and diplomats alike.

She opened her mouth to spin some excuse. Instead, the truth tumbled out.

"There's a man in my bed."

Henry's brows shot up. The smile evaporated. "Are you insane? Did you forget this was a prison? You could've dragged in some serial killer. "

He brushed past her before she could stop him, striding toward the bedroom.

. and froze in the doorway.

"No…" The word left him hollow.

The chamber trembled with silence.

Jessica pressed her hand against the satchel at her side, eyes darting between Henry and James. Something was wrong. Henry wasn't smiling anymore, wasn't teasing her as he always had. His expression was sharp, his gaze locked on James with calculation instead of warmth.

James moved first. His hand shot out like lightning, seizing Henry by the throat and slamming him into the wall. Stone cracked. Dust rained down in a thin veil.

Henry's eyes went wide. His hands clawed at James's arm, his mouth opening in a strangled gasp.

"James! Stop!" Jessica cried, panic burning her throat. She rushed forward, tugging desperately at his arm. "You're hurting him!"

But James's face was carved from fury, recognition burning in his scarred features. His voice rumbled low, ancient, guttural. "You are not human."

Henry thrashed, his voice breaking. "P-please. Jessica. help. "

Her chest wrenched. "He's Henry! Let him go!"

James ignored her. He slammed Henry against the wall again. The stone groaned under the impact. His voice was thunder. "Drop the façade."

The third strike shattered more than stone.

Jessica froze as cracks spiderwebbed across Henry's face. Not blood. Not bone. Glowing lines splitting like porcelain under a hammer. Her heart stopped.

Silver liquid welled from the fractures. thick, luminous, alive. It slid down his cheeks, poured across his throat, dissolving his clothes as it spread. Fabric turned to ash under its touch, reshaping into brilliant white cloaks trimmed in gold, embroidered with symbols older than any tongue.

Jessica stumbled back. Her stomach dropped. "No... no..."

The fractures sealed, and in their place stood a mask of flawless silver, a young, sculpted, eerily beautiful. But lifeless. Inhuman.

James's grip stayed firm, but the being. Sariel. no longer resisted. His reflective face tilted, calm, and serene. Angels did not need to breathe, sleep, eat, or feel emotions. They also did not feel pain.

His voice came steady, carrying weight enough to rattle the stone: "Azyrial. Still chained to your fury. Still blind."

Jessica's knees buckled. Her mentor. gone. The man who had guided her, laughed with her, cared for her like family. dissolved into something eternal and terrible.

James's hand trembled. Doubt flickered across his scarred features. For the first time since she freed him, he faltered. Slowly, he released his grip.

Sariel stepped forward, his cloak whispering against the stone. He turned to Jessica. Even behind that silver mask, she felt the weight of sorrow in his gaze. and chains wrapping around her chest.

"You have been seen," Sariel said. His voice rolled like a bell through the chamber. "By our law, you are already damned. Judgment will come for you both. It will not hesitate. It will not spare."

Jessica's lips parted, but no sound escaped. Her body shook, tears burning her eyes.

Then Sariel lifted his hand. His fingers curled into a simple gesture. small, intricate, deliberate.

Jessica didn't recognize it. But James did. His chest tightened, his eyes darkening with old recognition. It was a vow exchanged only between angels. love, kinship, compassion, and bound beyond language.

"You were his daughter," Sariel said softly. "Not by blood. By choice. He loved you. And now you are condemned, because of him."

The words shattered her. Her back hit the wall. Her heart screamed to deny it, but deep down, she knew. Henry was gone. Sariel was all that remained.

Sariel's voice sharpened, turning to James.
"You have damned my daughter in your waking anger. Protect her. If you are the angel of old."

The silver mask turned away. His wings unfurled. vast, blinding, streaked with fire and shadow. With a single beat, the chamber filled with wind and light as he hurled himself through the window. Glass exploded outward. Daylight swallowed him as he rose into the sky.

The silence that followed was unbearable. Glass glittered across the floor like tears.

Jessica pressed a trembling hand to her mouth, choking on a sob. He loved her. This being who was once her mentor, a father figure, her friend Henry. Now transformed into something of legends and myths, Sariel and he had still loved her as his own. And now, because of James, she was cursed to carry that truth into a world where even heaven turned against them.

James stood in the ruins, chest heaving, scars gleaming in the golden light. His hands shook, not from battle, but from the weight of Sariel's final words.

Jessica finally found her voice, broken and raw.
"What… what do we do now?"

James looked at her. His expression was unreadable. His voice low. "Now?" He exhaled, ragged. "Now I protect you. Whether heaven allows it or not."

And nothing would ever be the same again.

Jessica stayed pressed against the wall, her palms damp against the stone, her chest heaving as if she could squeeze sense back into the moment. Her mind reeled. Henry was gone, Sariel had damned her, judgment was coming. and yet the silence that followed was louder than the storm had been.

She dragged her hands down her face, smearing tears across her cheeks, trying to breathe. When she finally looked up, she froze.

James stood in the center of the ruined chamber, the broken window framing him in golden light. His bare broad chest glistening in the sunlight, his tattoos glowing faintly as if absorbing the light, leaving him still bare before her.

Her breath caught. His body was cut into perfection, every scar and line of muscle catching the sunlight in stark relief. There was nothing fragile in him. He looked carved, forged. a relic of something older than humanity, alive and standing in front of her. For one dizzy moment, she understood why people once mistook angels for gods.

The sight pulled her out of her spiraling grief and back into the present. The absurdity of it hit her first. the world had just been torn open, and here he was, utterly unclothed, illuminated like a statue in some cathedral alcove.

"Cloths!" she gasped suddenly, the word tumbling out. "You'll need clothes if we have to run. You can't go out into the world like. like this."

Her face flushed, though she forced herself to keep her tone practical. "I'll check Henry's room. He… he won't be back for them."

James tilted his head slightly, a faint, unreadable shadow crossing his expression. He said nothing, but the slow dip of his chin was enough.

Jessica moved to the door, her hand on the broken frame. She hesitated, her throat tight, then glanced back at him. His scars glowed faintly in the fractured light; his eyes steady on her.

"Don't leave," she said softly. "Not yet."

He gave her a single, silent nod.

The door clicked shut behind her, sealing her into the long stone corridor. Jessica took three steps before her body betrayed her.

The sobs hit like a breaking dam. She staggered against the wall, pressing her forehead to the cold stone, her shoulders shaking with the grief she had fought to hold back. It tore out of her in ragged breaths, Henry's laugh, Henry's voice, Henry's care echoing through her memory, all now tainted by silver and light and judgment.

She let it come. She had to. Because once it was gone, she would have nothing left to give to grief.

At last, her body quieted. She wiped her face hard with both hands, smearing away tears until her cheeks burned. A long inhale steadied her. She straightened, pulling her shoulders back, setting her jaw.

The woman who pushed forward wasn't the same one who had stumbled from that chamber. She had to bury this, lock it away, and move.

Jessica forced her steps quiet as she turned down the corridor, until Henry's chamber door loomed ahead. She paused only once more to smooth her hair, to press the last of her tears into her sleeve. Then she gripped the latch and pushed her way inside.

Chapter 14. The Hunt Begins

Henry's Room

The corridor outside her quarters felt impossibly long. Jessica's footsteps barely whispered against the stone, yet every sound seemed magnified, as if the monastery itself listened. When she reached Henry's door, her hand lingered on the iron latch. The wood felt cold, as though the room already knew he was gone.

She slipped inside.

The air smelled faintly of parchment and cedar oil, clean and crisp, like a library carefully tended. The room was unnervingly immaculate. Books were aligned on shelves so precisely their spines looked like soldiers in formation. Artifact cases sat sealed, each labeled in Henry's tidy script. Maps and documents were tucked into neat stacks with weights pinning the corners.

But near the window, on a small table, the discipline faltered.

Jessica's gaze caught on photographs in mismatched frames. Her throat tightened as she crossed the room.

A much younger Henry, hair darker, stood in front of an Anatolian temple with the sun at his back. Another photo caught him mid-laughter in a Moroccan market, a vendor draping scarves across his shoulders like a king. And then. her breath hitched. there was one of *them*.

She and Henry, shoulder to shoulder in the dust of a Mayan tomb. Their headlamps hung loose around their necks, faces smeared with dirt, grins stretching wide as crates of recovered artifacts filled the space behind them. She remembered the adrenaline, the sting of sweat in her eyes, the rush of victory.

Her knees weakened. Henry. Sariel. whatever he was. had been this man too. He had stood beside her in triumph, cracked jokes over bad meals, guided her through impossible puzzles. That had been real, hadn't it? It *felt* real.

Jessica lowered herself into the chair, fingers trembling as they brushed the frame. Her reflection shimmered faintly in the glass, fractured by dust and age. She let the weight of it press down for a moment, then forced herself upright.

There wasn't time. Not now.

Clothing the Stranger

Jessica turned to the wardrobe, each drawer sliding with mechanical precision. His clothes were as orderly as the rest of his life. pressed shirts, folded trousers, clean socks rolled into pairs. She dug through, pulling what she thought might suit James.

Dark denim jeans. They'd hang loose but would last. A grey button-up, soft with wear. A jacket in muted charcoal, formal enough to blend but plain enough to vanish in a crowd. Steel-toed boots. practical, heavy, reliable.

The scent of Henry clung faintly to the fabric: soap, faint earth, a ghost of incense. It almost undid her. Her eyes blurred, and she clenched the jacket tight, willing the emotion away.

She folded the clothes into a bundle and gathered them to her chest.

On her way out, she paused once more at the table. Her fingers hovered over the photograph of them in the tomb, the two of them immortalized in dusty joy. A sob pushed at her ribs, sharp and insistent. She swallowed it whole, turned, and slipped back into the hall without looking back.

Dressing for the World

Her chamber was a ruin of broken glass and faint sunlight. James stood where she had left him, framed by the fractured window, his body still bare. The light turned his skin into a sculpture. every scar and line sharpened into something both terrible and beautiful.

Jessica thrust the bundle into his arms. "Here. You'll need these."

He dressed with quiet efficiency. The jeans clung awkwardly at first, the fabric foreign, but he adjusted quickly. The shirt stretched across his shoulders; the jacket hung loose but serviceable. The boots were heavy, but he laced them tight with sure hands.

Jessica watched in silence. When he finished, he looked at her. His voice was low, deliberate.

"James," he said. "My name is James."

The name landed between them like a stone. Jessica's breath caught. She had heard Sariel call him something else, something older, heavier. But this. this she could hold onto.

She nodded. "Alright, James. Let's get you out of here."

The Ascent from the Depths

They left the chamber behind. The corridors felt darker than before, the weight of centuries pressing from every side. Jessica moved quickly, guiding him through narrow stairwells and storage passages. Her knowledge of the rhythms of the place steadied her. the bells that drew monks to prayer, the silences that emptied halls.

Dust clung to the air, stirred by their passing. The smell of old stone and extinguished candles filled her lungs. Every creak of wood and shuffle of boots sent her heart pounding faster.

James followed without question, silent and immense. His presence pressed at her back like a shadow too large to ignore.

Jessica's mind wouldn't still. She didn't know if anything was chasing them, if heaven's eyes had already turned toward them. But every step carried the same urgency: *move, don't stop, don't look back.*

Through the Gates and into the Modern World

The iron gates loomed ahead, their black bars crowned with sharp points that caught the pale dawn light. Two monks stood near the entry, speaking softly, their voices muffled by the rattle of a supply cart climbing the hill.

Jessica's pulse hammered. Timing was everything.

When the cart rolled forward, she slipped into step beside it, gripping one of the crates as if she were just another worker. James fell into place behind her, shoulders lowered, head angled down.

The monks didn't even glance their way. The hinges groaned. The gates opened.

And then they were through.

Air rushed in, sharp and free, scented with pine and damp earth. Jessica exhaled for the first time in hours. But she didn't slow. Freedom was fragile, and it could be snatched back in a heartbeat.

Into the City

The monastery shrank behind them as they descended the hill, its towers swallowed by cypress and stone. The road wound downward, each step carrying them further from the sanctity of walls that had become a prison.

The air warmed as the sun rose higher, trading incense for the earthy scent of soil and wildflowers. Birds stirred in the trees, their calls sharp against the hush of morning. The weight of judgment lingered behind them, invisible but unbearable.

By the time they reached the edge of the countryside, the land had softened into fields and scattered villas. A faded bus stop crouched beneath the shade of a cypress tree. Its bench sagged, the paint cracked, but it promised escape.

Jessica bought two tickets to Rome with hands that still trembled. James lingered behind her, silent, watching.

When the bus finally arrived, its engine growled like a beast reluctant to wake. She climbed aboard; the satchel clutched to her chest. James followed, settled beside her with a quiet weight.

As the bus pulled away, Jessica pressed her forehead to the glass. The monastery vanished into the hills, leaving only the road ahead.

Rome awaited. sprawling, noisy, alive. A place to hide, at least for now.

But Jessica knew the truth: whatever hunted them would not be stopped by gates or distance.

Chapter 15. Streets in Motion

The bus ride down from the hills felt longer than it was.

Jessica sat angled toward the window; her cheek nearly pressed to the glass as the monastery's walls slipped out of sight behind a winding bend. White stone receded into a haze of cypress groves and terraced fields until it seemed the place had never existed at all. just a dream abandoned in the mountains.

The road narrowed, snaking along ridges that dropped into shadowed valleys. Each curve tilted the bus enough to make her grip the leather strap on the seat in front of her. The engine rattled and groaned, fighting gravity with every descent. The air smelled of old diesel, dust, and too many unwashed coats pressed together.

Around her, passengers shifted restlessly. Two monks murmured prayers, beads clicking softly in their hands. A mother hushed her coughing child, rocking him against her shoulder while the older man across the aisle muttered in irritation. Behind her, someone whispered a joke in Italian that drew a stifled laugh, sharp and out of place in the heavy air.

Jessica kept her gaze outward, but her ears tracked everything. Every cough. Every shuffle. Every voice. The satchel resting in her lap felt heavier than it should. the weight of journals, sketches, fragments of Adam's writing pressing against her thighs like secrets made solid. She hugged it closer, fingers tightening on the strap, certain everyone could feel its pull if they looked at her long enough.

The bus jolted over a pothole, throwing her forward. The satchel thumped hard against her chest. She swallowed the spike of panic, forcing her hands to steady. Just a bag, she told herself. Just notebooks. No one else knows.

Besides her, James hadn't moved.

At first, she thought he was simply being cautious. Then she looked closer. His hands were clamped so tightly on the metal seat frame that the steel groaned under the strain. His amber eyes flicked constantly. from the fluorescent lights overhead to the rattling windows, to the glowing phone in the man's hand across the aisle. His chest rose too fast, shallow. His jaw locked hard.

He wasn't bracing for pursuit. He was bracing for the *bus itself.*

"The ground moves," he muttered, low, meant only for her. "Yet no horses pull it. The air shakes with fire, but I cannot see the flame."

Jessica blinked, realization slamming into her. *He doesn't know. He has no frame of reference. He's been in darkness for centuries… and the world went on without him.*

The man across the aisle swiped at his phone, a glow spilling across his face. James stiffened, pupils narrowing, every muscle taut. "They all carry mirrors that speak," he whispered. "And they are bored by them."

Jessica leaned closer, lowering her voice. "It's not sorcery. It's… technology. Machines. Tools. Like quills and parchment, only faster. Stronger."

James stared at her, confusion hardening into distrust.

"They're safe," she pressed. "Ignore them. Trust me."

For a long moment, he didn't move. Then his grip on the seat eased slightly, though tension still rippled through him like coiled wire.

The silence of the monastery still clung to her like a second skin. the echo of her own footsteps in long corridors, the whisper of prayers, the oppressive weight of stone and secrets. Out here, the noise of the world was overwhelming, chaotic, almost alien.

And then Rome appeared.

First as a smudge of rooftops glittering in the distance, then swelling into a sprawl of stone, glass, and asphalt that devoured the horizon. Streets braided together in endless streams of traffic. cars, buses, scooters weaving recklessly, horns blaring, voices shouting. Laundry flapped from balconies. Vendors barked their wares from crowded corners. The city moved with a pulse, alive in every direction.

James pressed stiffly against the window, staring with something between awe and suspicion. His amber eyes tracked the blur of headlights and neon, the graffiti streaks across concrete. "This is no empire I have known," he murmured. "It is a city of ghosts. Fire without flame. Gods of ink and light."

Jessica gripped her satchel tighter. She should have felt relief at being swallowed back into the ordinary world. Instead, unease coiled deeper. Every stranger's face seemed sharp. Every movement in the crowd is deliberate. The city was too alive, too aware as though it somehow knew what she carried with her, and what she had freed.

The brakes squealed as the bus lurched into the terminal, a hiss of steam rising into the night air. Passengers muttered, shoving past each other to spill into the street.

Jessica stayed seated, waiting until the last body brushed by her. Her knuckles whitened around the satchel strap.

When she finally stepped down the iron steps, the city struck her like a wave.

The smell hit first a hot asphalt, gasoline, roasted chestnuts, all layered with the sour tang of unwashed bodies pressed too close. Then the noise the horns blaring, mopeds whining like angry wasps, vendors shouting, pigeons scattering in a clatter of wings. Voices crashed together in Italian, English, Arabic, and French a dozen tongues blending into a restless hum.

James stepped down beside her, stiff and silent. The rain slicked his shaved head, running down the scars hidden beneath his shirt. His eyes scanned every sign, every car, every glowing window like they were weapons waiting to strike.

Jessica pulled her satchel tight and forced herself into the current of people. Every brush of contact sent paranoia sparking through her. Did they know? Could they feel it? That she wasn't just carrying notebooks and sketches, but something far more dangerous?

Above her, neon signs flickered. Graffiti sprawled like wounds across walls. Scooters cut sharp lines through traffic, their riders balancing impossible loads. Somewhere, a radio blared music loud enough to rattle glass.

Jessica pressed forward, her pulse heavy. The monastery's silence was gone. Rome swallowed her whole.

And James a stranger to this world, a man seemingly in darkness for centuries out of time, chained too long in darkness. Opened his eyes for the first time and stared at the city like it was both miracles and betrayals.

Chapter 16. The New World

Into the Crowd

The streets swallowed them the moment they stepped off the bus.

Rome surged like a storm without rain. a torrent of movement, voices, and light. Vendors shouted from stalls lined with pyramids of fruit and stacks of bread still steaming from their ovens. Scooters screamed between cars. Neon signs flashed in broken colors across wet cobblestones. Jessica tightened the strap of her satchel and pushed forward into the current.

James didn't move.

He stood at the curb, shoulders squared, eyes sweeping over everything as though he'd stepped onto a battlefield. The flashing billboards, the humming electric wires, the crush of humanity. every detail froze him. His gaze burned amber beneath the glow, unblinking, predatory.

"Come on," Jessica urged, grabbing his wrist and pulling him into the river of people before they were trampled.

The crowd folded around them, brushing and bumping, strangers speaking languages James didn't recognize. A man cursed as James's shoulder clipped him. A woman laughed too loud on her phone. Teenagers shoved past, trailing cigarette smoke and echoes of music from a tinny speaker.

To Jessica, it was life. To James, it was shadows of an era long forgotten, and chaos remained, but alien to him now.

"These faces…" His voice was low, meant only for her. "They do not see one another. They move like shades in the underworld."

Jessica darted a glance at him. His expression was carved from disbelief, not wonder. "They see," she countered quickly. "They just don't *look*. That's how you survive here. Keep moving. Don't stand out."

But James stood out no matter what she said. He moved like a soldier. every step rigid, every turn of his head sharp, cataloguing alleys, rooftops, every reflection in shop glass. He wasn't walking through a city; he was walking through enemy territory.

Idols in the Sky

A car horn split the air. James's head jerked, eyes narrowing at the glowing screen that towered above them. a perfume ad projected onto the side of a building.

A woman's face loomed ten feet tall, flawless, her lips parting in silent promise before sound spilled from a speaker overhead, breathy and false.

"False gods," James muttered, his lip curling. "Painted idols in the sky."

Jessica caught his arm before he froze in the middle of the street. "It's advertising," she explained quickly, tugging him forward. "People pay to put their faces up there to sell things."

"Sell… faces?" His tone was edged with contempt, as though the word itself was a curse.

"Close enough," she said, forcing a dry laugh.

He gave the screen one last glare before following, though she could feel the tension radiating from him.

Iron Beasts

They turned down a narrower street where old stone walls closed in, graffiti curling like vines across their surfaces. Laundry hung from rusting balconies above, dripping with the morning's rain. Somewhere, a radio blared from an open window. a voice singing in Italian, drowned out by the metallic screech of a tram.

The tram burst into the street with a grinding roar, sparks spitting from its rails, heat and electricity rolling off it in waves. James stiffened instantly. His body shifted, stance widening, hand twitching for a weapon he didn't have.

Jessica saw it too late. She seized his wrist, forcing his arm down before he lunged. "Don't," she hissed. "It's just transport. People ride it to cross the city."

His eyes stayed locked on the tram, burning with suspicion. "And you trust this? This… iron beast that screams and breathes smoke?"

"I don't trust it," she admitted, matching his intensity. "But I use it. That's the difference."

The tram shrieked past, showering sparks, then vanished into the night.

James exhaled once, but his jaw stayed tight. When his eyes finally left the tracks and returned to hers, something softened. For the first time since stepping off the bus, he moved in step with her instead of against the tide.

The City's Pulse

They walked for blocks, the chaos thinning as the streets narrowed and the traffic gave way to courtyards and alleys. Rome's pulse was everywhere: water rushing through ancient drains beneath the streets, voices rising from cafés, bells tolling from unseen towers.

Jessica's nerves vibrated with every sound. A door slammed shut. she flinched. A dog barked in the distance. her stomach twisted. The crowd thinned but her paranoia thickened. Every shadow seemed too deep. Every passerby lingered too long.

Beside her, James's focus never wavered. His head turned to track reflections in windows, the shift of cloth in alleys, the way footsteps echoed behind them. He walked close enough that his arm brushed hers, his presence solid and deliberate.

It wasn't comfort. It was a promise.

Ghosts in the Flesh

They stopped briefly at a fountain where the water ran clear over marble chipped by centuries. Jessica bent to splash her face, needing the cold to steady her. When she straightened, James was staring at the crowd again. men in suits, women in skirts, a beggar crouched near the fountain's edge.

"They are ghosts," James murmured. "Flesh that moves without seeing, without knowing. They pass each other as if they do not exist."

Jessica followed his gaze. To her, it was ordinary life. To him, it was a nightmare.

"They're alive," she said softly. "But sometimes… it doesn't feel that way."

His eyes turned toward her, and she saw it hidden beneath the suspicion, beneath the alienation a focus and unflinching readiness. An old, inexhaustible alertness to fight, to protect, to endure.

His hand brushed against hers. Not for comfort. Not by accident. Deliberate.

Jessica looked away quickly, her pulse thudding in her ears. For now, it was enough.

The streets of Rome were alive with ghosts.

Jessica pulled James through the rain-slicked avenues, weaving between scooters, vendors, and strangers moving too fast to notice them. To her, the chaos was ordinary. Exhausting, dangerous, but familiar. To James, it was something else entirely.

Every headlight, every horn, every shifting shadow drew his eyes like blades being drawn. He walked stiffly, his amber gaze scanning rooftops, alleys, neon signs. The tram that screeched by made his jaw tighten, his hand twitch as if ready to strike. A billboard flickered with a giant face, perfume spray bursting across the night sky, and he muttered darkly, "Painted idols. False gods."

Jessica caught his wrist before he froze in the middle of the sidewalk.
"Not gods. Ads. It is noise. Ignore it."

His glare softened only slightly, but the mistrust stayed. He had been in darkness for centuries, and now the world pulsed and screamed around him. She guided him forward anyway, her satchel heavy against her hip, her heart heavier.

They reached a quieter block near Trastevere, the noise thinning to the occasional bark of a dog or the roll of thunder over the city. Jessica found the apartment door, fumbling with the old iron key until it scraped open.

Inside, the space was small, dim, smelling of dust and old stone. Neon bled through the curtains, painting the walls with restless color. James stood at the window, arms crossed, eyes never leaving the streets below. He was still coiled. Still listening for dangers she could not see.

Jessica sat at the table, the encrypted phone cold in her palm. The satchel lay open beside her, Adam's sketches and fragments spilling across the wood. None of it mattered if she could not find someone she trusted.

She scrolled slowly through her private list.
These were not Henry's names.
Not the monks.
Hers.

Pulled from years in the Bureau. From favors and debts buried deep. She had never used them unless there was no other choice.

And tonight, there was no other choice.

Her thumb stopped on one name.

Thomas Kali.

They had never met in person. He was not a friend. He was not even a colleague. He was a ghost in the network, whispered about in rooms with no recordings, where people lowered their voices. Known for solving problems no one else could touch. Dangerous. Unforgiving.

Reliable.

Her stomach tightened as she pressed call.

One ring.
Two.
Three.

"…You have reached a restricted line," a distorted voice said. "State your name. If I know it, I will decide whether you are worth answering."

Jessica exhaled slowly. She should have hung up.

Instead she said, "Jessica Trainer."

A pause.

Then the distortion dropped.

"Oh," the man said flatly. "Well. That explains a lot."

Her brow furrowed. "Explains what?"

"That the last six hours of my life lit up like a forensic symposium." A dry snort. "Every buried relay I monitor started screaming at once."

"You were expecting me?" she asked carefully.

A scoff came through the line. "Expecting you specifically, no. Expecting something ugly, yes."

She hesitated. "How did you know something was happening?"

"Jessica, the digital traffic spike alone lit up like a…"

"A Christmas tree?" she offered.

The line went quiet for a moment.

Then, more serious. "An inferno."

Her stomach dropped. "So you have been tracking it."

"I track everything that threatens to break the world in half," he said. "Until five minutes ago, I just did not know it was you standing in the blast radius."

Jessica tightened her grip on the phone. "I need help, Kali."

"You always do," he said mildly. "The difference is whether you are about to cost me sleep or blood."

"I am serious."

"That is never in question."

A brief pause followed. Then, sharper. "Are you alone?"

Her gaze drifted to the bedroom door. Closed. James lay inside, silent, impossibly still.

The truth pressed against her throat like a blade.

"Yes," she lied.

Silence stretched.

Not empty.

Evaluating.

"Mm," Kali finally said. "That was not the answer I was listening for."

Her pulse spiked. "Will you help me or not?"

"Tomorrow night," he said. "Trastevere district. No trail. No tails. If either rule breaks, the meeting fails before it begins."

"You will be there?" she asked.

"I said I would find you," he replied. "That does not mean I will stay."

The line cut.

Jessica lowered the phone slowly, staring at the blank screen. Neon flickered across the walls, painting the room in restless color. The hum of the refrigerator felt loud enough to betray her heartbeat.

Her hand hovered over the satchel before curling into a fist. She turned toward the bedroom door, her chest tight.

She had just lied to the one man who might be able to save her.

She was not alone.

And she knew, with a cold certainty, that Thomas Kali knew it too.

Chapter 18. Midnight in the Citadel

While angels pursued their prey with patience and precision, something else stalked the world. Something older than many of them, and far less forgiving.

He was known now as Markus HailFire. It was not the first name he had worn, and it would not be the last.

Once, he had been only a man.

Long ago, he had crossed paths with something far greater than himself. A being of fire and wrath had torn his victories from him in a single night. Armies had burned beneath skies the color of molten copper. Kingdoms had collapsed into screaming ash. The air had tasted of sulfur and hot iron. Markus had crawled from the ruin scarred, breathless, half-blind with smoke in his lungs and blood in his mouth.

He had risen changed.

What followed was a story only he carried, sealed behind silence and buried beneath the steel in his voice and the weight in his presence. Some whispered he had bargained with demons. Others said he had stolen a fragment of heaven itself. The truth belonged only to him. It lived in the tight line of his jaw, in the scars hidden at his collar, in the way men instinctively lowered their eyes when he entered a room.

Whatever had remade him, it had left him more than human.

Now, under the name HailFire, Markus commanded an empire that bent science, war, and faith into his will. The world believed him untouchable because no one alive remembered what had once brought him low.

But Markus remembered.

The Status Report

The chamber was quiet, suspended high above the city like a throne carved from glass and shadow. Rain streaked down the exterior windows in thin silver veins. Far below, the lights of the metropolis pulsed like a living circuit board, restless and sleepless.

Markus sat at his antique desk, its hand-carved surface dark with age and oil, its edges worn smooth by the presence of men long dead. With a faint metallic click, the center seam split open. Three massive vertical screens rose from within the desk and ignited the darkness with cold blue light.

The central feed sharpened into focus on Dr. Kyra Meinhardt.

Her laboratory hummed faintly behind her with the sound of machines that measured things no scripture dared to name. Her lab coat was immaculate. Her hair was bound in a severe knot at the base of her skull. The light reflected sharply off the lenses of her glasses.

"Status report," Markus said.

His voice was quiet. It carried anyway.

Dr. Meinhardt began at once. "Reaper combat readiness is at optimal threshold. Biomedical systems remain stable. Neural interface response times fall within six milliseconds of projected peak performance. All deployed assets remain synchronized to command relays."

The side screens spilled into motion as she spoke. Biometric telemetry scrolled in violent green pulses. Combat simulations replayed in stark monochrome. Reapers moved across burning streets and shattered corridors with inhuman efficiency. Matte black armor absorbed the light. Gunmetal joints flexed with machine precision. Veins of crimson illumination pulsed faintly beneath plating like artificial blood.

Their helmets bore no face. No eyes. Only the faint suggestion that something human had once existed beneath composite alloys.

"Celestial trace," Markus said.

Dr. Meinhardt shifted the display. A faint waveform rose into view. Thin. Irregular. Almost timid.

"Still present on the female," she said. "Barely measurable. Residual transfer only. As you predicted."

"For months," Markus said softly. "A whisper instead of a beacon."

Dr. Meinhardt hesitated. The silence stretched just long enough to be noticed.

"There has been a change," she said.

The waveform detonated across the screen.

It erupted upward in violent spikes of light, shattering the previous scale. Data surged. Alarms whispered through the lab beyond the feed.

Her breath caught. "The moment she removed the seal, the celestial output exceeded all predictive thresholds. The signal is no longer dormant. It is active."

Markus leaned forward. Light climbed the planes of his face and washed the scars at his collar in pale silver.

"And its source?"

Her fingers moved quickly. The display shifted.

The name appeared.

James.

The chamber fell silent except for the distant thunder of rain against glass.

Markus stared at the screen.

Then he smiled.

"Change the priority," he said.

Dr. Meinhardt stiffened. "From the carrier?"

"Yes," Markus replied. "She was never the prize. Only the container."

Her hands moved across the console. The target marker slid away from Jessica Trainer and locked onto James.

"Primary asset confirmed," she said. "Target is to be retrieved intact."

Markus rose from his chair. The floor seemed to hold its breath.

"What she carried was only the echo," he said. "What she freed is the origin."

For the first time, uncertainty touched Dr. Meinhardt's face. "Then she was not the lock."

"No," Markus said. "She was the key. And now the door stands open."

Change of Target

Azazel waited in the shadow near the chamber wall like a statue carved from violence.

The fortress no longer trembled at his presence. It had learned to fear in silence. The metallic scent that followed him drifted faintly through the chamber and clung to the air like the ghost of old blood.

Markus did not look at him.

"Your target has changed," Markus said.

Azazel's head tilted. Cable-like tendons beneath his neck tightened. The rebuilt cobalt eye within his mask sharpened as the new designation synced internally.

James.

"Orders?" the distorted voice asked.

"Track. Do not engage. He is to be unspoiled."

Azazel inclined his head in flawless obedience. Motion rippled through his armored frame as he turned and vanished into the dim corridor beyond.

The Corridor

The doors sealed behind him with a hiss, leaving Markus to the shadows. Azazel's pace was steady, heavy, his presence filling the long stone hallway with weight.

It didn't take long before voices reached him. two security men, their conversation carried by the echo of the hall.

"…I'm telling you; Markus isn't right. A warlord, sure. but why keep that woman doctor, so close? And that fucking little kid… why does he let a child trail through the halls like some… ghost?"

The second guard hissed sharply, "Shut up. You don't speak like that here. Not about him."

Too late.

Azazel's sensors had already locked onto them. The air seemed to vanish, the corridor narrowing into silence as he closed the distance. Neither man saw him until the shadow fell over them.

The first guard. the talker. turned just in time to feel a hand clamp around his throat. Flesh crushed against metal. Azazel lifted him easily, boots kicking uselessly in the air. His cobalt eye glowed faintly as he studied the struggling man, tilting his head with slow, predatory curiosity.

Then came the sound.

SNAP.

The guard's neck broke cleanly.

POP.

The base of his skull tore from the spine in a grotesque crack. His body sagged instantly, limp, before Azazel released him. He crumpled to the polished floor, head twisted at an impossible angle.

The second guard froze, eyes wide, hands rising slowly into the air. His breath came shallow, terror pouring from every pore as Azazel turned his gaze on him. For a long, unbearable moment, the hybrid's eye flickered, iris narrowing, as though calculating his worth.

Then, without a word, Azazel turned away. His katana shifted at his back as he continued down the hall, the sound of his steps swallowing the silence.

The surviving guard collapsed against the wall, heart hammering. He fumbled for his comm, voice trembling. "Unit down... Sector C hallway. Send... send a crew now."

His eyes lingered on the corpse, bile rising in his throat. His hands shook violently, and in a hoarse whisper he admitted the truth aloud:

"Yup... I pissed myself."

The streets pressed close around them, brick walls leaning inward like they had waited centuries to trap someone. Jessica's boots struck wet cobblestone in sharp, even rhythm. James moved ahead of her in near silence, no more than a ripple of shadow.

Behind them came the sound again.

Click.
Click.
Click.

Mechanical. Measured. Wrong.

"They are closer," Jessica said under her breath.

James did not answer. He slipped into the narrow gap between two buildings, his coat brushing the stone. She followed, shoulders scraping damp brick.

A voice burst from the earpiece she had stripped off a fallen Reaper earlier. Harsh consonants crackled in a language she did not know. Then one clean word in English.

"Advance."

Jessica's hand dropped to her Glock. "We should. "

The first one hit from above.

Steel slammed into stone as a Reaper dropped from a fire escape. James pivoted without looking. His elbow rose like a blade and smashed into the joint beneath the Reaper's visor. Metal buckled. The impact twisted the attacker sideways into the wall. Bone snapped beneath armor. The Reaper twitched once and went still.

Another was already lifting his rifle.

Jessica fired twice. Ping. Ping. The rounds sparked off chest plating.

James surged forward. He caught the rifle by the barrel, wrenched it down, and drove a knee into the armor seam at the hip. The joint failed. His next punch crushed inward under the rib plate. The Reaper folded with a wet, internal crack and slammed face-first into the ground.

James did not wait for movement.

He brought his boot down onto the back of the helmet.

The skull shattered inside the shell.

They ran again before the body finished twitching.

The alley spilled into what remained of an open market square. Overturned tables lay scattered. Crates of rotting fruit burst beneath their feet. The air reeked of rain, citrus, and spilled wine.

A Reaper charged across the square.

James vaulted a vendor table in one motion, caught the edge of a cart, and used it as a springboard. He came down behind the charging figure and twisted its head violently to the side. Cervical plating split. The spine snapped. The body dropped mid-stride.

Another attacked from the right.

Jessica fired again, rounds skidding sparks across its shoulder. She ducked as the Reaper swung.

James seized the attacker by the throat plate and drove him backward into a stone column. The impact cracked the pillar and crushed the Reaper's chest inward. He jerked once, then went limp.

Jessica had seen trained fighters before.

She had never seen execution like this.

"Where did you learn to fight like that?" she shouted, weaving between shattered stalls.

"Later," James said. He dropped into a low crouch and swept two Reapers off their feet with a single spinning kick. "Keep moving."

The square funneled into a long stone corridor lined with empty archways. Above them, shapes moved.

More Reapers.

They poured down from the ledges like spiders.

Jessica's pulse spiked. "We are boxed in."

James ran two steps up the wall and launched himself sideways. He crashed into the first Reaper midair. The impact drove both of them over the arch and into the street below. Stone exploded on impact.

Jessica fired upward, forcing the others back. She heard the heavy thud of boots as James landed beside her again.

No wasted breath. No wasted motion.

They ran.

By the time they reached the bridge, Jessica had counted four separate ambushes in less than ten minutes.

And then two more Reapers dropped directly in front of her.

One lunged.

Jessica slid low and kicked hard into the side of its knee joint. The armor buckled. The Reaper stumbled forward with a grinding mechanical shriek.

She rose and drove a heel into its visor.

The glass fractured. The unit reeled backward.

The second Reaper raised its weapon.

It never fired.

James hit it from behind. His hands locked under the helmet rim. He twisted.

The neck snapped.

Before the first could recover, James pivoted and drove a crushing strike into the exposed back plating at the base of the spine.

The Reaper folded in half with a violent crack.

Both bodies hit the stone.

Dead.

Jessica stared for half a second longer than she meant to.

It had been too easy.

On the bridge's far side, James seized the last Reaper standing and slammed him against the railing. The unit fought wildly. James ripped the glowing wrist display free and crushed the arm backward until the elbow bent the wrong way. He scanned the screen as data poured across it in red streams.

His voice dropped. "It is not me."

Jessica caught her breath. "What?"

"They are not hunting me," he said. "They are hunting you."

A Moment to Breathe

They slipped into the collapsed shelter of an abandoned tram station. Rusted rails vanished into darkness. Water dripped in slow, hollow echoes from broken pipes overhead. Steam hissed from a ruptured valve along the wall.

Jessica braced a hand against the concrete, lungs burning.

"Okay," she said between breaths, "you are going to tell me what the hell that was. Unless you have secretly been auditioning for So You Think You Can Kill Me."

James kept his eyes on the tunnel mouth. His shoulders barely rose as he breathed. "Not important right now."

"Not important?" She barked a shaky laugh. "You fight like you have been doing it since the Crusades."

She froze. "Oh God. Have you been doing it since the Crusades?"

Something flickered across his face. Regret, ancient and heavy.

"You do not want the truth," he said.

Jessica pulled her phone from her cargo pocket and scrolled to a name under a lock icon. "I know a place. It is risky. Not exactly on the tourist map, but it might buy us a few hours."

James finally looked at her. "And?"

"And I have someone who owes me," she said, pressing call. "If they answer, we get our breather. If not..."

She glanced down the tunnel as the faint insect-like clicks echoed again.

"...we keep running."

The streets pressed close around them, brick walls leaning inward like they had waited centuries to trap someone. Rain ran in silver sheets down shattered stone. Water pooled in the ruts between cobblestones. Garbage floated at the edges of the walking lanes. The city did not sleep here. It watched.

Jessica's boots struck wet stone in steady, punishing rhythm. Every step jarred up her legs and into her spine. Her lungs burned in time with her movement. James moved ahead of her in near silence, more presence than body. A shadow that bent the darkness around it.

Behind them, the sound followed.

Click.
Click.
Click.

Metal shaped to mimic pursuit.

Her phone vibrated hard against her ribs.

She did not slow as she answered.

The call barely rang once before the voice hit her ear. It was low, rough with sleep deprivation and chronic irritation. The kind of voice that lived on caffeine and paranoia.

"This is not a good time, Jess."

"It is never a good time with you," she said. Her eyes cut toward the alley mouth where distant metal scraped against masonry. "I need a roof. Now."

A pause crackled across the line. Keys clacked faintly beneath his breathing.

"This about Trieste?" he asked.

"It is about you still owing me for Trieste."

Silence stretched just long enough for tension to take hold. Then the sharp sound of a chair scraping back.

"You called earlier than expected," Kali said. "That tells me something broke."

"Everything broke."

A bitter laugh hissed through the receiver. "I am watching surveillance from four districts right now. Your friend is turning armored soldiers into salvage."

Jessica's jaw tightened. "You are tracking us."

"I track catastrophes," he snapped. "You keep reclassifying yourself."

"That is not helping."

"Neither is the walking extinction event you are escorting."

She slowed under a dripping archway. Rain slithered down broken statues overhead.

"We need to disappear," she said. "For six hours. That is all I am asking."

A keyboard rattled violently. Screens flicked in reflected light across rain puddles ahead of her.

"You are dragging half the underworld behind you," Kali said. "Every kill your friend makes raises the temperature of the net. You are radioactive right now. You do not get to hide. You burn."

Jessica stopped.

Her breath came out thin and sharp. "You owe me your freedom. I could have left you locked in a container bound for a black site in Albania, and I did not. I pulled you out through a sewer grate with gunfire at my back."

Another pause.

This one heavier.

"You should not have done that," he said quietly.

"I did it anyway. Now you repay the debt."

"Jessica, you do not understand what you brought into my world."

Her voice turned cold. "I understand very clearly what I brought into yours. I brought you a chance to be alive. Now choose whether you help me stay that way."

Rain hammered down harder. The sound swallowed the city.

The call clicked.

A second later, her phone chimed.

Six numbers.

A grid coordinate.

"You have six hours," Kali said. "After that, the spot is burned beyond memory."

"Generous as always," she said.

"The building is near the hostel where you were headed," he continued. "Do not trust the front entrance. Do not look like you belong. Follow the drains."

The line went dead.

James glanced back at her.

"It is never simple," she said. "But it will keep us breathing."

They moved again.

The hostel stood crooked beneath a dying neon sign that flickered weak red through the rain. Paint peeled in pale curls along its brick facade. A revolving door wheezed on every turn. Cigarette smoke bled through the cracked seams around the glass panels.

Inside, heat slapped against their soaked clothes. The air was thick with old smoke, wet fabric, sweat, and secrets that refused to evaporate. A rattling fan stirred nothing but stale breath. People lingered in the corners. Hunched bodies. Hidden faces. Conversations whispered into cupped hands. Nobody looked too long.

Jessica did not break stride.

They passed the front desk without a word. Down a narrow stairwell that creaked and protested with every step. Each footfall sent shivers through the corroded railing. The basement smelled of mildew and forgotten alcohol. Broken crates lined the walls. A single exposed bulb swung from a frayed wire above.

James scanned every surface. Concrete. Rust. Mold. Water stains shaped like crawling things.

"Cozy," he said.

Jessica did not answer. She stopped at a raised seam in the floor and struck it twice with her heel.

The wrong stone shifted.

Cold air exhaled upward from the dark.

They descended.

The undercity swallowed them.

The air fell thick and heavy around their lungs. Water ran in shallow channels along the floor. The smell of sewage pressed into the back of the throat until taste followed it. Gray shapes skittered along the edges of vision. Rats. Things that were not rats.

James's eyes adapted almost instantly.

He saw movement where Jessica saw shadow.

Forms clung to masonry like muscle wrapped in skin not meant for light. Carnal silhouettes layered with deformity and hunger. Watching.

"No sudden moves when we arrive," she said quietly. "He owes me, but he does not trust me."

James inclined his head once.

The tunnel widened into a chamber lit only by a red lamp that bled color rather than light. The glow pulsed faintly nhu a slow heartbeat.

A short, thick man stood beneath it. Long coat. Flat cap. Hands buried deep in his pockets.

He did not speak at first.

His eyes never left James.

"Had I known you were bringing company," the man said at last, "I might have staged something impressive."

Jessica glanced around the bare chamber. Wet stone. Rusted racks. A single metal chair. "You outdid yourself."

That earned the faintest twitch of a smile.

"Good to see you alive," he rasped. "But I am lit up in every encrypted forum from here to Odessa. That means you and your shadow have six hours. No more."

"It is enough," she said. "I will balance the ledger."

He scoffed. "You never fully do."

He turned.

Pressed a code into the wall.

A slab slid aside.

"Be safe," he said. "Very bad people are looking for you. I now have to become a rumor again."

He slowed as he passed James. Their eyes locked.

A Predator eyes met a digital predator eyes.

Then the man vanished into black stone.

The safe house was deliberate.

A cot.

A rolled mat.

A bucket toilet.

A gravity shower bag suspended from pipe.

Crates of water.

Cans of food.

A locked case of ammunition.

Jessica opened the crate. Counted the supplies. Efficient. No excess.

She reloaded her Glock with practiced hands.

Set it down.

Exhaled for the first time in hours.

Silence pressed in. No engines. No radios. No mechanical clicking.

Only the red lamp hum.

James stood against the wall with arms folded. Watching the doorway. Listening to the tunnel breathe.

Jessica turned the valve on the shower bag.

Water fell in thin, icy threads.

She stripped her jacket. Then her shirt. Then her boots.

Cold shocked across her skin. Stole the heat from her muscles. She braced one palm against the wall and let it wash the blood and grit away.

Soap scraped across sore arms.

She glanced once over her shoulder.

James had not moved.

He did not need to turn to know where she stood.

Did not need sight to know the shape of her presence.

What stirred in him now was not simple desire.

It was older.

Dangerous.

It rewrote the inside of a man.

He stayed where he was.

Listening.

Guarding.

Choosing restraint again.

Above them, the storm broke open across Rome.

High above the city, where no human eye could reach, two figures stood within the storm.

Their presence bent the air around them. Winds shifted course without warning. Rain slowed, hesitated, then resumed its fall. Lightning curled around the edges of distant clouds and never touched them. Feathers stirred without sound. The world below moved on in ignorance.

"His chains are broken," one said.

The words were not spoken with a mouth. They existed as weight between them.

The second did not answer at first. His gaze remained fixed on the glowing scars of the city far below, where mortal light bled through water and shadow.

"They were not meant to break this way," the second said at last.

"No," the first replied. "They were not meant to break at all."

Silence gathered between them, pressed tight with memory older than empires.

"How did he escape?" the first asked. "The seals were absolute. His prison was woven into stone and vow and blood. No mortal hand should have undone it."

The second's eyes shifted, following a moving thread below. "And yet one did."

"A woman," the first said. "A fragile thing of breath and bone."

"She was not meant to be a key," the second answered. "She was only meant to be nearby."

"Proximity does not shatter eternity," the first said coldly. "Interference does."

The second turned his face now. The storm reflected silver across his eyes. "Do you truly believe he forced his way free?"

"What else could it be?"

"Choice," the second said.

The word struck like a tremor between them.

The first angel's feathers stiffened. "You suggest we allowed it."

"I suggest," the second replied slowly, "that he did not tear his chains apart. He stepped through a door we believed was sealed forever."

The storm roared lower around them.

"He is free," the first said. "Then the judgment must proceed."

"And if he does not become what he once was?" the second asked.

The first's gaze sharpened. "He is Wrath. That was not a title. It was a function of creation."

"And yet," the second said quietly, "the one who now walks in his form refuses that mantle with every breath. Did you see the way he fought? Not for conquest. Not for rage. Only to protect."

"Protection does not erase what he is."

"No," the second agreed. "But it reveals what he fears becoming."

The first angel's hand drifted toward the hilt of a blade shaped of hardened starlight. Its edge glimmered with a cold purity that had ended worlds before.

"He is unbound," the first said. "Fear will not stop what destiny commands."

"And yet fear stopped him from slaughter," the second replied. "Fear stayed his hand when he could have erased the street. Fear kept the city standing."

A long silence followed.

The storm turned.

"But the woman," the first said again. "She carries him now. Through her, he moves unseen. Through her, he learns restraint. That makes her complicit."

The second's voice softened. "Or it makes her the reason the world still stands."

"You hesitate," the first said.

"I observe," the second answered. "And what I observe is not Wrath awakening. What I observe is a god hiding inside the shape of a frightened man."

The blade's light dimmed slightly.

"If he falls again," the first said, "we will not wait."

"And if he rises instead?" the second asked.

The first did not answer.

The storm swallowed them where they stood. Their forms dissolved into light and vanished into clouds and rain.

Below the City

In the red glow of the undercity, Jessica pulled on clean clothes with shaking hands. Water dripped from her hair onto the concrete floor.

James stood with his back to her, unmoving, listening to threats the human world could not hear.

Above them, heaven had paused.

And judgment, once absolute, now hesitated.

Chapter 20. Confessions and Sins

The red lamp's glow painted the walls in muted bloodlight. The only sounds were the faint drip of water in the tunnels and the soft, steady trickle from the shower bag.

Jessica stepped out from the alcove, drying her arms with the hem of her shirt. Damp strands of hair clung to the back of her neck. The cold had settled deep into her skin, but she welcomed it. It kept her grounded.

James had not moved from his place against the wall.

His head rested against the stone now. His arms hung loose at his sides. His eyes were closed.

For a man like him, sleep was not indulgence. It was surrender. Something the body took when the mind could no longer refuse it. There was no tension in his fingers. No readiness in his posture. The sharp vigilance she had seen since the monastery was gone.

He was fully unconscious.

She lingered near the edge of the alcove, watching him breathe. Slow. Even. Too human for what he was supposed to be.

Her world no longer made sense.

Everything she had believed in had been stripped apart within days. Angels. Reapers. Eternal prisons. A man who moved through centuries as if they were rooms in a hallway.

She had spent her life chasing hidden truths. But this truth did not live on paper. It lived in flesh and fire.

James shifted suddenly.

Not a waking movement. A full-body jolt.

His back arched an inch off the wall. Breath shuddered violently from his chest. A sound tore loose from his throat, broken and wordless. Then he fell still again.

Jessica straightened in alarm and crossed to him in two strides.

"James," she breathed.

No answer.

His pulse hammered beneath her fingers when she pressed them lightly to his wrist. Too fast. Then slower. Then steady once more.

Relief eased her shoulders.

Until the light changed.

The markings along his arms began to glow.

Not bright.

Not violent.

A low amber pulse moved through them like a buried heartbeat awakening under skin. The light deepened with each breath he took.

Jessica froze.

She had not touched him yet.

The tether activated on its own.

Something shifted in the air between them. Pressure without wind. Heat without flame. The sensation wrapped around her chest and tightened.

His body jerked again.

Stronger this time.

The amber light surged.

Jessica did not decide to reach for him.

Her hand moved without intent.

The moment her fingers made contact with his skin, the world collapsed.

There was no falling.

No drifting.

She was seized and pulled down through a tearing vacuum of sensation. The red room shattered into fragments of color and sound that stretched and dissolved into nothing.

Her breath vanished.

Her body ceased to exist.

She was no longer in the safe house.

She was inside him.

Darkness unfolded in vast layers around her, not empty but structured, arranged by impossible geometry. Enormous corridors spiraled outward like the inside of a living cathedral. The air vibrated with restrained power so heavy it bowed her senses.

A distant, titanic heartbeat pulsed through the void.

Not human.

Not divine.

Something bound between both.

Light ignited along the walls in slow-moving currents of molten amber. Symbols moved within the glow, ancient and shifting, forming and reforming with purpose she could not understand.

A voice moved around her.

Not sound.

Presence.

You should not be here.

Jessica turned, but there was no body attached to the warning. Only awareness pressing against her from all sides.

"This is inside you," she whispered into the dark.

The heartbeat answered.

She felt him then.

Not the man lying unconscious in the undercity.

Not the fighter who had broken steel and bone in the streets of Rome.

This was something deeper.

Older.

A vast presence restrained and folded inward upon itself.

She stepped forward.

The chamber responded.

Light surged violently along the floor in spirals of fire and shadow as something immense shifted beneath the surface of the reality she stood upon.

Fear slammed into her.

Not of what he was.

Of what had been done to him.

The chains were here.

Not physical.

Conceptual.

Forged of vow and judgment and enforced obedience.

They were broken.

Not torn.

Unlocked.

The truth hit her like a blade.

He had not escaped by force.

He had been released.

And something had answered that release.

The pressure slammed into her chest.

Her senses fragmented.

The darkness folded inward.

And James's presence surged toward her consciousness for the first time.

Not awake.

Not aware.

But reaching all the same.

The Soul Chamber opened fully around her.

And Jessica fell into the heart of the Horseman.

Darkness swallowed her.
Then she opened her eyes to a light.

Not the forgiving kind that warms the bones or curls like sleep around the eyes. This light was cold and distant, planetary in scale. It fell from places too far away to name and onto depths that had never known morning. It spilled across a space so vast it dismantled the mind's sense of measure, a cathedral whose ceiling receded until it became an absent sky.

The air tasted damp and mineral-heavy, salted by stone and old water. It pressed against her skin with the quiet, crushing weight of the deep ocean.

Jessica stood at the mouth of a colossal tunnel.

The walls were not smooth planes but living relief. Black rock and fossilized bone folded together in shifting layers as if the carving had not finished deciding what it wanted to be. Figures crowded the surface: warriors frozen in endless war cries, angels carved mid-ascent with every feather preserved, other things with too many joints and too many eyes folded into anatomies that refused the law of the human form.

When she looked away, they tilted.

Watched.

Steps rose ahead of her. They were built from skulls and shattered femurs mortared with mineral and old gore. Condensation slicked every surface. The hollowed eye sockets reflected her in fractured repetitions, a procession of ghost-images with no pupils.

Her boots rasped against calcium. The sound was intimate and wrong.

Cold clung to her braids. Moisture gathered on her lashes until it weighed like grief. The air hovered near fifty degrees and sank straight into the bone. Each breath left her mouth in pale vapor that lingered too long before thinning.

Time had gone thin here. It did not move so much as hesitate between instants. The drip of water stretched its intervals. Heartbeats became metronomes without a clock.

She lifted her wrist out of habit.

There was no watch. Only skin. Only memory.

She swallowed. The air tasted like old pennies and limestone.

She climbed.

The sound of her ascent vanished into immensity, consumed as if the place refused to acknowledge motion. When her palm brushed the wall for balance, the relief was slick and faintly warm. Not sun-warm. Hoarded heat. Trapped heat.

The carved eyes followed.

In one panel, an angel knelt with his head bowed. His crown was a ring of thorns forged from ribs. In another, a city burned without flame as its inhabitants folded into the ground like sand pulled by retreating tide.

At the summit, the stairs narrowed into gates so tall they felt like a lie.

Iron and blackened gold bowed under their own weight. Rivets the size of skulls stitched the plates together. The panels were carved into impossible depth: coronations, titans in chains dragged by winged executioners, kneeling supplicants crushed beneath ascending light. Language before language swarmed the margins, symbols that her eyes felt but could not translate.

A pale pulse of light throbbed through the seam like a sleeping heart.

She set her palm to the metal.

Cold bit deep into her bones. For one breath, nothing happened.

Then the gates moved.

They groaned inward with the sound of stone grinding on bone. The seam tore open like the earth remembering it had once been molten. Wind poured out rib-deep, heavy with salt, silt, and old prayers cooked down into iron.

Beyond lay the chamber.

A central granite path threaded forward between vast pools of black water. Waterfalls descended in silent curtains from immeasurable heights, silver sheets stitching darkness to itself. No roar, only pressure. A winter surf heard from miles away.

Mist curled low and clung to her skin like a second breath. Somewhere overhead, a chain creaked once and sent its vibration slithering through the stone and into her bones.

She thought the pools were empty.

Then she saw the faces.

Hundreds. Thousands. Pressed just beneath the glassy surface. Eyes wide to their last shock. Mouths locked into shapes that had begun as screams. The waterfalls poured over them without ripple. The liquid was not water.

It was transparency.

A held moment of agony.

Her throat tightened. "Oh my God."

Her breath scattered across the chamber and vanished into congregation.

She stepped onto the path.

With each footfall, the pools brightened as if the light rose to witness the trespass. The eyes below tugged at her balance. She kept to the centerline, hands flexing to remind herself she was still anchored to a body.

The path widened.

The throne awaited.

It was grown, not built. Femurs and scapulae fused with obsidian, seams soldered with iron-red slag. Dried blood had sunk so deep into the structure that the stone drank it as pattern. Spines arched to form the arms. A vaulted ribcage rose to make the back.

Upon it sat a sovereign of judgment.

Eight feet tall. Armored in white and gold so intricate it appeared alive. Plates interlocked like living scripture. Sigils braided across him, every mark a written sentence that had already passed verdict.

The mantle was not fabric. It was hammered light folded into obedience.

A blade like a slab of frozen sky stood driven point-first into the steps before him. Granite fractured outward in frozen spiderwebs.

He leaned forward.

Not movement. Declaration.

Jessica stepped once. Twice.

Then the helm turned.

Amber ignited beneath shadow.

James's eyes.

And not his at all.

Steam sighed from between the plates. A sound rolled from within the armor, slow and deep as thunder hunting for a canyon.

"Do you seek blood and pain here?"

The voice did not travel to her ears. It collapsed directly into her chest. The pools tightened. The faces flexed.

"You are forbidden to be here."

Color bled into the waterfalls. A faint pink that darkened into red. The chamber darkened with it.

He rose.

Stone groaned like awakening mountains. Inscriptions across his chest inhaled light and exhaled dim.

He stepped down.

Once. Twice.

He stopped at the final step.

He did not need to come closer.

"Who are you?" she managed.

A consideration.

"The question is not who I am. The question is why you have entered a chamber where ruin remembers its first hunger."

She thought of chains dissolving in her hands. Of steam. Of a man who called himself James.

"I had to know," she whispered. "If this is you."

Long silence.

Then quietly, which meant the chamber bent closer to listen:

"I did not bring you here. This place remembers every cost. Your breath is measured against fires that outlived the world."

He reached back. Closed his hand around the throne.

Bone shrieked. Stone complained.

The throne shattered like a broken spine.

Rust-powder fell like dead snow.

"You must leave before this hunger consumes you."

Gravity inverted.

"NOW."

The chamber hurled her.

Cold seized her sternum.

The world tore.

Jessica jolted upright on the sleeping roll, lungs clawing for air.

The red lamp hummed.

The tunnel stank of wet limestone and rust.

James remained against the wall, eyes closed, breathing steady.

Twenty minutes.

Inside the chamber, it had been hours.

Her hands shook.

The Chamber was not gone.

It stood behind the world now.

Waiting.

Somewhere far beneath Rome, a crushed throne remembered what it was and refused to mend.

And something that was not James lifted amber eyes toward the seam between worlds.

It would not be the last time she walked there.

And not the last time it looked back.

The red lamp breathed softly in the corner.

Its glow barely touched the edges of the room, leaving most of the space swallowed in shadow. The stone still held the cold of the Chamber. Jessica could feel it in her bones, in the backs of her knees, in the hollow beneath her ribs where fear liked to hide after it had been awakened.

She lay on the thin sleeping roll and stared at the ceiling she could not truly see.

The faces in the water had not left her.

James had not moved from the wall, but she felt him wake long before he stirred. There was a tension to his stillness now, not the vigilance of a sentry, but the awareness of something that had already been touched.

Her.

He crossed the small space without a word and lowered himself beside her, back to the wall, knees drawn slightly, posture restrained by habit rather than comfort.

She glanced at him, surprised.

He did not meet her eyes.

She shifted closer without deciding to. The movement came from elsewhere, from some quiet pull beneath choice. "It's cold," she murmured, lightly, because the truth beneath it felt too heavy to speak aloud.

James did not stop her.

When she settled against his side, warmth slid slowly into the places the Chamber had hollowed. The scent of her skin reached him, clean and human and unbearably alive. He closed his eyes once, briefly, as if bracing against something.

The red lamp hummed.

Water dripped in the tunnels like a distant clock.

"I think I went somewhere," Jessica said at last. "Not in the tunnel. Somewhere else."
She hesitated. "It felt more real than this."

James's jaw tightened.

She tipped her head to look up at him. "You knew."

His breath left him in a slow exhale. "I was afraid you had."

"Well," she said softly, "you better start being honest."

Silence stretched between them, taut as wire.

"It is not a place meant for mortals," he said at last. "What you saw belongs to what I was before I learned how to hide."

Her voice was steady, but her hands trembled against his sleeve. "The souls in the water. The throne. The thing wearing your eyes."

He nodded once.

"That is my sentence," he said quietly. "Not my prison. My sentence."

She drew a slow breath. "James… what are you?"

His gaze drifted to the darkness where the tunnel bent away. "I am not one of the four."

Her heart stuttered.

"I am the origin of the story," he continued. "The calamity that learned how to fracture itself into symbols so the world could survive knowing it existed."

Her mouth went dry. "You're saying the legends… the riders…"

"Are masks," he said. "Worn so the truth would not be named."

A quiet terror bloomed in her chest. "The souls in the Chamber… all of them…"

"Are bound to me," he said. "Not as captives. As consequence."

She pressed her palm against his chest without thinking.

His breath caught.

"When I sleep," he said, voice roughening, "they wake. When I rest, they remember through me. Every death I carried becomes weight again."

The red light shuddered faintly.

She did not pull her hand away.

Instead, she leaned into him and wrapped her arms around his torso, holding him as if the act itself were prayer. "You're not alone anymore," she whispered. "I saw you. I didn't break."

His eyes closed.

For the first time in centuries, he let himself be held without chains.

Her lips brushed the hollow beneath his jaw, just once. Warm. Real.

The moment her skin touched his, the tether answered.

Heat surged beneath his scars. Gold laced through the ink of his tattoos in slow, luminous pulse. Amber flared in her eyes like a caught sunrise.

Neither of them breathed.

The connection struck like a bell rung inside both their chests.

Not desire.

Not romance.

Recognition.

For an instant, they were not two bodies in a borrowed shelter beneath Rome. They were two halves of a mechanism older than gods. Frost and flame. Judgment and mercy. Destroyer and the only thing that could still reach him.

The kiss that followed was not hunger.

It was collapse.

Their mouths met softly at first, uncertain, as if the universe itself hesitated with them. Then the tether tightened, and the contact deepened with something that had never learned how to be human.

James pulled back. not in rejection, but in fear.

"If I surrender to this," he said hoarsely, "I risk becoming the thing the world chained me to forget."

"And if you don't," she replied, steady as iron, "you stay trapped in it forever."

They held each other's gaze.

Two forces balanced on a single breath.

Above them, far beyond stone and rain and sky, something ancient shifted its attention.

The tether had awakened.

And for the first time since the dawn of wrath, the Horseman was no longer alone inside his fire.

Chapter 23. Our Love is Our Bond

The kiss did not break.

It deepened slowly, as if the air itself were thickening around them. What began as heat became gravity. What began as want became inevitability.

Jessica felt it first in the quiet places inside her chest, where the ache lived long before her body answered. Her hands slid into the fabric of his shirt not to pull him closer, but because distance suddenly felt unlivable. James's breath caught against her mouth, restrained, trembling with a control that was fraying one millimeter at a time.

The red lamp pulsed.

Once.

Twice.

The tether tightened.

Her palms flattened to his chest, right over the slow, dangerous rhythm of his heart. When she pressed there, his tattoos answered. Gold fire crept through black ink in branching veins, slow and deliberate, like something waking after centuries of sleep.

Jessica inhaled sharply.

"James…" His name left her like a confession.

He broke the kiss only long enough to rest his forehead against hers. His voice was low, almost reverent. "If we cross this line… it will not be only the body that changes."

Her answer was not spoken.

She leaned in and kissed him again, and the tether chose for them.

The Chamber roared without sound.

Heat surged through both of them, not burning, but *reshaping*. Jessica's breath stuttered as sensation bloomed under her skin in ways touch alone could not explain. Every place he held her felt amplified, as if her nerves were no longer hers alone. She could feel him feeling her.

And he could feel her inside him.

Not flesh.

Essence.

James's control finally fractured. His hands slid into her hair, not rough, but desperate, anchoring himself before the Horseman following the pull tore forward. Her body molded to his instinctively, every movement guided by that invisible current binding them together.

This was not conquest.

This was convergence.

When they finally collapsed onto the sleeping roll together, it was not with urgency but with surrender. Clothing fell away not as urgency, but as necessity. Skin to skin was not heat alone now. it hummed, alive with light beneath the surface.

Their union was slow.

Deliberate.

Not driven by hunger alone, but by recognition.

Jessica arched into him as the tether brightened, her breath breaking against his throat as every sensation unfolded twice: once in flesh, once in flame. James moved as if memory guided him, as if some ancient truth was guiding his hands which no human lifetime had taught him.

With every motion, the Horseman retreated.

With every breath she took, James returned.

Their release did not come violently.

It came like a breach in a dam that had been holding back an entire sea.

Light burned quietly through their bodies as they shattered together, not in explosion, but in collapse, trembling, undone, held inside something far larger than themselves.

When it was over, Jessica lay against his chest, trembling with aftershocks that were not entirely physical.

James held her without fear.

For the first time in his existence, he held without judgment.

"You didn't save me," he whispered into her hair. "You reminded me I was still here."

Her lips curved faintly at his throat. "Same thing."

They stayed like that for a long time.

The red lamp dimmed.

The tunnels exhaled.

The world dared to continue turning.

Eventually her breathing steadied. Her fingers traced the faint glow of his tattoos as the gold faded back into ink. "We didn't just… connect, did we?"

"No," he answered quietly. "We sealed something that was already written."

She lifted her head enough to look at him. "What did we seal?"

His amber eyes met hers without hiding now. "My choice."

Her expression softened. "To be what?"

~ 183 ~

He hesitated.

"To remain James."

Silence settled again.

Not empty.

Full.

After a while, her gaze drifted toward the broken window where moonlight spilled across stone. Her thoughts turned slow, heavy with questions that now felt older than her fear.

"What was Rome like," she asked gently, "when you were here the first time?"

His body stilled.

Not in fear.

In memory.

The tether responded instantly.

The chamber dissolved.

Fire replaced stone.

And Jessica opened her eyes inside a city that was screaming.

The room had gone still again.

The red lamp hummed softly in the corner, its glow muted now, as if even it were weary. Jessica lay against James's chest, listening to the slow, steady rhythm beneath her ear. His warmth was real. Solid. Anchoring.

For the first time since Rome, since the tunnels, since the blood and running and revelation, nothing chased them.

She traced the faint edge of one of his tattoos with her fingertip, following the black line as it curved over muscle and disappeared beneath fabric. It no longer glowed, but she felt it under her skin anyway, like an echo that had not yet finished speaking.

"Do you ever forget things?" she asked quietly.

His breath shifted beneath her cheek. "No."

She lifted her head slightly to look at him. His eyes were open now, amber faint but steady in the low light. There was no fear in them. Only memory.

"Not even after all this time?" she asked.

"Especially not after all this time," he answered.

She hesitated. The question had been forming since the moment the bond had settled between them. Since the echo of fire in her blood. Since she had seen the edge of what he carried.

"Do you remember Rome?" she asked.

The change in him was instant.

Not physical at first. Not a flinch or a tightening of muscle. It was something deeper, something that moved behind his eyes like a storm cresting just below the surface.

"I never forgot Rome," he said.

His voice was quiet.

Too quiet.

The air between them thickened.

Her fingertip was still resting against his chest when she felt it. The tether did not ignite this time. It *opened*. There was no surge, no heat. Just a sudden, vertiginous sensation of depth beneath her touch, like pressing against glass and realizing it was no longer there.

James's breath left him in a slow, controlled exhale.

"You should not see this," he murmured.

But it was already happening.

The bond tightened, not as fire now, but as gravity.

Jessica felt the room tilt.

The red lamp stretched into a smear of crimson.

His heartbeat slowed beneath her palm, not stopping, but changing rhythm, becoming something older, heavier. She tried to pull back, suddenly afraid of where the question had led them.

She could not.

The tether had chosen.

James's eyes met hers one last time, and in them she saw it. Not the Horseman. Not wrath.

Memory.

The world inverted.

Stone replaced shadow.

Heat replaced cold.

And Jessica fell, not into dream, not into vision. but into the living past of a man who had once burned Rome to cinders.

Chapter 24. Blood in the Sand (The Mortal Destroyer)

The red lamp's glow painted the walls in muted bloodlight. Jessica lay against James's chest, the warmth of his body a steady anchor after the storm they'd just shared. Her cheek rose and fell with the rhythm of his breathing, the quiet thud of his heartbeat grounding her in the silence.

Her eyes traced the shadows on the wall. She hesitated, then asked softly, "Do you remember Rome?"

The question pulled at something deep inside him. His chest shifted beneath her, his breath slowing, as if the weight of centuries was settling over him.

And then she was no longer in the red-lit hideout.

It wasn't like falling asleep. it was like being dragged through time. The scent of damp stone was gone, replaced by hot, dry air thick with the stench of blood and sunbaked sand.

Rome.

The Colosseum roared with the voices of tens of thousands. The sound was not joy, not sport. it was hunger. A city's collective craving for blood.

In the center of the arena stood James no not James, Azyrial. Alive in every sense. His body glistened with sweat, his bare chest streaked with crimson. His pale white hair caught the sunlight like a halo, though his amber eyes were molten and merciless. In his hands, twin blades dripped with gore. Around him lay the broken. warriors, slaves, beasts, criminals, innocents dragged in for spectacle. Their blood turned the sand black beneath his feet.

The crowd called him *Lupus Aureus*, the Golden Wolf. Not for his hair, not for his eyes, but for the way he stalked, toyed, and killed. He was not a gladiator. He was a predator loosed into their cage.

Jessica felt her stomach twist as the bond tethered her to him. She could feel what he felt, the power, the blood-lust, the hunger deep within him. This was not a battle for survival. It was blood for its own sake.

Three gladiators were set loose against him, scarred men armed with tridents, nets, and short swords. They circled him cautiously, sweat already beading on their brows. Their faces shrouded in helmets and armor.

Azyrial smiled to himself under his own helm.

He allowed them to land the first blows. A slash opened across his shoulder, another along his ribs. Blood ran, the crowd roared and he laughed inside his own mind. Jessica could feel it: the thrill of the sting, the pleasure in the pain. He made the fight a performance, every strike calculated to excite the mob. And then, like lightning, he ended it.

One throat opened with a single slash, spraying crimson across the sand. Another man screamed as his trident was twisted from his hands and driven through his chest. The last gladiator fell to his knees, net tangled around him. Azyrial drove his blade into the man's mouth and wrenched it sideways until his head split open like fruit.

The crowd erupted.

And so, it went. Fight after fight. Day after day. Weeks into months. Opponent after opponent fell to his blades, his fists, his bare hands. He left the sand painted red, until the lanista's refused to risk more men against him. The doors to the arena closed, but his hunger remained unsated.

So, they turned to beasts.

Gates rattled open, chains clanged, and from the dark tunnels came lions, their golden eyes flashing in the sun. Tigers slunk low, shoulders rippling. Bears lumbered forward, their growls shaking the sand. Even a rhinoceros was driven into the arena, armored with leather straps and goaded by barbed spears until it bellowed fury.

The crowd rose as one, ecstatic, eager to see the monster torn down.

But the beasts hesitated.

Jessica felt it through the bond. their instincts, primal and raw, recoiled from him. They sensed what the men had not. This was no human prey. This was something older, darker. The lions circled wide, unwilling to charge. The tiger's ears flattened, snarling but refusing to come closer. Even the rhino, maddened and bleeding from its handlers' prods, slowed when Azyrial's gaze met its own.

The crowd howled at their reluctance, frenzy igniting as fear spread through the animals.

And then Azyrial moved.

He leapt, blades flashing, meeting the lion's pounce head-on. The beast's roar ended in a wet gurgle as steel split its throat, blood spraying in a crimson arc. The tiger lunged, too slow. Its skull caved beneath his heel, spine snapping as he wrenched its body sideways.

The bear charged, claws raking his flesh. He laughed through the blood, crimson streaking down his chest, before he drove both blades deep into its ribs and tore them outward until the beast collapsed in a broken heap.

The rhino came last, horn gleaming, a wall of flesh and fury. The arena shook with its charge. The crowd screamed in ecstasy. Jessica's breath caught up in her breath, she could *feel* the impact through the bond. But at the last instant, Azyrial shifted aside, dragging his blade across its flank, ripping a trench of blood along its side. The beast stumbled, turned, and charged again. This time, he met it head-on. His broadsword plunged beneath its jaw, splitting bones and hiding until the horned beast toppled, earth shuddering as it struck the sand.

Silence fell for a heartbeat.

And then the Colosseum erupted.

Tens of thousands screamed his name, their frenzy louder than thunder. They did not see that the beasts' fear had been their warning. They only saw their monster triumph again.

Jessica staggered in horror, clutching her chest as the bond forced her to feel it all, the roar of the crowd, the spray of warm blood, the savage pleasure that flooded Azyrial as he stood among the mangled bodies of the dead. He did not fight for survival. Not for gold. Not for glory.

He fought only to end life.

When even beasts could not slake his hunger, Azyrial went deeper. into the underground pits, where law did not reach. Here, there was no ceremony, no trumpets or laurel crowns. Only stone walls sweating with damp, torches guttering in stale air, the stench of piss and blood heavy enough to choke. Fights ended not when men yielded, but when bodies no longer moved.

Azyrial thrived here.

Jessica felt it. the ecstasy of violence, the freedom of it. He crushed skulls with his bare hands, ripped jaws from faces, tore limbs from sockets as though men were dolls. He killed with weapons when they were given but killed just as gladly without. His rage was not selective. it fell on all who crossed him.

The crowds of the pit. thieves, killers, the dregs of Rome. cheered louder for him than the Colosseum had. They did not see a man. They saw something beyond man. And still, his lust was never satisfied.

When the pits grew silent, when no one would face him, he took to the streets.

Predators came for him in the alleys a wide variety of cutthroats, mercenaries, Praetorians drunk with their own untrusting

~ 192 ~

intentions. None survived. Their bodies were left mangled as warnings: spines twisted, skulls crushed, eyes plucked and placed in their hands like coins for Charon. Even the Praetorian Guard whispered of him in fear.

Women in the pleasure districts tried to entice him. Some thought his beauty meant softness, others thought to tame him. He silenced them all. He did not care foe delicate things, and some were silenced with a blade, some with his bare hands. Their cries were brief. His lust was not for flesh. Only blood and death.

Rome called him champion. But in truth, it had crowned its destroyer.

And then came the day.

Paraded on horseback, laurel on his brow, flowers raining from balconies, children crying out his name. Jessica felt a bile rise in her throat. They adored him, worshipped him, unaware they were feeding their own death.

The emperor welcomed him into marble halls. Priests blessed him. Courtiers smiled. And when asked what reward he desired, Azyrial's lips curled.

"I am not your champion," he said. His voice cracked like thunder through the chamber. "I am death."

The words had barely left him when he moved.

It was faster than sight. A blur of shadow, steel, and smoke.

The boy turned with his wooden sword raised playfully. "Daddy"

His voice choked into silence as his head separated from his shoulders. Blood fountained in a sudden arc, splattering across the emperor's face and gilded robes. The child's head landed at his father's feet, glassy eyes staring up in shock.

The emperor flinched taking a single step back, his cry strangled by horror. The Queen's scream pierced the chamber.

The emperor turned to his queen, "Guards!!!...Guar..." and then the emperor's own head was gone, severed cleanly in a single, fluid strike. It toppled into his lap, eyes still wide with disbelief.

The Queen rose half from her throne, still shrieking, before the blade carved sideways. Half her head slipped free, her upper skull and face sliding off with a wet, sloppy sound that struck the marble floor. Her lower jaw and tongue twitched grotesquely atop her still-seated body before collapsing in a spray of gore.

The guards froze, paralyzed, horror etching their faces. Their weapons trembled in their hands, their discipline broken by the sheer speed and brutality of the massacre.

Azyrial turned toward them, shadows bleeding from his armor, his broadsword dripping in deep crimson blood that looked black. His eyes blazed like two molten suns.

Looking at the pretorian guards, "It is too late to run, it is too late to hide." he said, his voice calm as the grave. As the soldiers regained themselves and attacked. Azyrial, stabbed his blade deep into the marble floor and fire erupted in all directions consuming them all, turning flesh and bone to ash. Azyrial reveled in the screams as men died.

And then the killing began.

The palace fell first.

Then the city.

Jessica's mind reeled. She smelled the burning wheat of the markets, heard the screams of mothers trapped in collapsing villas, saw idols toppled in temples as priests coughed blood through their prayers. She was drowning in his rage, in his blood lust, in his endless hunger for death.

Rome burned. Rome bled. Rome died.

And still he walked the streets openly.

The Colosseum, once belonged to the citizens of Rome, his arena became his altar. Tens of thousands screamed his name in terror, trapped inside the city as the walls sealed with shadow. He slaughtered them where they stood. Families clutched each other as fire rained from the sky. By dawn, the Eternal City was ash.

And still one place stood. The place where they prayed to their false gods.

The temple.

"There is no sanctuary here among your false god" he said. His voice was not loud, yet it filled the streets. "There is no peace."

He raised his sword. Shadows swelled. More lives snuffed out like candles in the wind. The innocents ran through the streets, fires consumed everything, and as the panic ensued.

Rome was gone.

Chapter 25. Holy Ground (I Am Death)

Azryial walked from the palace into a city instantly shaken, and filled with an growing fear that surged as he emerged from the fires of the palace into the light.

The crowd that had once cheered him and showered him with praise, who had rained laurel and petals upon his head now stood frozen. Their eyes tracked the three severed heads tumbling down the marble steps, rolling until they rested at their feet. The emperor. The queen. The boy.

For a heartbeat there was silence. Then a single woman screamed.

"Come and see…" His voice echoed across the forum, riding the heat that rose from burning marble.

What followed was not battle. It was annihilation.

He descended into them like a storm given flesh, his broadsword carving arcs of black fire. Men fell screaming, their bodies halved at the waist. Arms spun skyward, blood spraying in hot ribbons across the cobbles. Women collapsed clutching infants who were silenced in the same stroke. Dogs barked madly before their heads were crushed underfoot. Horses reared, shrieking, trampling their handlers before his blade cut them down in swaths. Pigs, goats, oxen. beasts of burden and food alike. were slaughtered as casually as men.

The city dissolved into chaos. Statues toppled. Market stalls erupted in flames. Villas collapsed as fire licked along their timber frames. The air reeked of smoke, blood, and charred flesh. Jessica's lungs tightened within the vision, her mind drowning in the stench, the screams, the madness.

Azryial did not rush. He walked. Slowly. Deliberately. Each swing of his sword was precise, savoring the end of another life. His steps cracked marble beneath him. Every death was his offering, every scream his hymn.

The Praetorian Guard tried to rally. Shields clanged together; spears lowered in disciplined formation. For a moment, it seemed Rome would resist. Then he fell upon them.

Shields splintered like kindling. Spears snapped in two. Helmets imploded as his blade crushed skulls, fusing steel and bone into a single ruin. Their battle cries turned to gurgling screams, their formation breaking apart as men scattered only to be cut down from behind.

Rome broke.

The people fled where they could, trampling one another in their desperation. Some sought the Tiber, throwing themselves into the dark waters to escape fire only to drown in chaos. Others ran blindly through the alleys, only to find his shadow already ahead of them.

But most, most ran to the temple.

The bells tolled wildly, cracked bronze groaning in protest as priests pulled the ropes until their palms bled. "Sanctuary!" they shouted. "Sanctuary in Zeus's temple!!"

Thousands flooded its steps. senators, slaves, courtesans, beggars. Mothers pressed babes to their breasts. Fathers dragged children by their hands. The wide doors groaned open and swallowed them into darkness lit by fevered candlelight.

And still he followed.

The weight of his steps shook the marble as he climbed. Sparks hissed from the edge of his blade dragging across the stones. Ash drifted from his shoulders like a black snowfall. His shadow stretched ahead of him, swallowing the temple doors before he ever touched them.

The doors groaned, as he pressed against it, they had barred them. Azyrial used his massive blade to cut deep into the door frame, severing the bar lock, he clenched his massive, gauntleted hand and with a single punch, the doors exploded.

Inside, the nave was packed to suffocation. The air was thick with incense, sweat, and terror. People huddled shoulder to shoulder, pressed into pews, sprawled across the aisles. Priests and acolytes stood at the altar, voices breaking as they chanted prayers that could not be heard above the sobbing of children. The light of a thousand candles flickered across pale, wide eyes.

Jessica felt it all. The claustrophobia. The hopelessness. The taste of fear so thick it clung to her tongue.

And then his presence entered.

~ 199 ~

Azryial's shadow spilled across the nave, drowning the candles in its wake. The air bent around him as though recoiling. People shrank back, pressing against columns, whispering prayers that turned to choked sobs when they realized prayer could not save them.

He strode to the altar, each step echoing like a tolling bell. His voice followed, deep enough to rattle the marble itself.

"You think you're HIS children?" His words rolled like thunder. "You don't deserve Eden. You're just meat. And when I am present. look upon thee... Death."

He raised his sword high. The blackened steel, veined with molten cracks, caught firelight in hellish glow. His body radiated to the finality.

The end had come.

Then the air shifted.

A gust swept through the cathedral, carrying with it the scent of clean air, as if the heavens themselves had opened a window. The candles flared. Incense smoke parted.

She descended.

Ramiel, wings of blinding white folding behind her as her boots touched marble soundlessly. She knelt in the aisle, head bowed in complete submission, her feathers trembling in the firelit gloom.

"Mighty Azryial," her voice was steady, but low, the weight of sorrow threaded through every syllable, "please leave this holy place. Leave this city. Spare the innocents…please, I offer my life in exchange and find satisfaction in taking my life."

Her head snapped up, eyes flashing with sudden fire. "Be satisfied!" The words cracked through the chamber like a whip; a command heavy with desperate authority.

Jessica felt Azryial's hatred coil like a serpent. His gauntleted fingers clenched around the hilt. His stance shifted. The air thickened with intent, with rage, with the inevitability of the strike.

He raised the sword higher.

But before Ramiel could move, Jessica did.

She didn't understand how, only that she had to. A young child clutched to her as she broke away and walked up to the massive beast before her.

Her steps were silent, her body not wholly her own, but her will was. The bond carried her forward, pulling her into the heat, into the suffocating pressure of his presence. Every instinct screamed to turn back, but something stronger, something eternal, drove her on.

Her fingers touched his armored forearm.

Instantly, the world changed.

Azryial froze. His head snaped down to her. His eyes left the angel in submission, and the alter he was about to sever into pieces. His eyes fell on her touch. Jessica's fingers lingered against the black plates, and though they were not hers, she could feel them as if they were. Beneath the armor she felt it: an ocean of rage, the weight of souls beyond counting. Yet beneath it all…something else.

His eyes widened. A golden arcing of energy flared and cracked.

Light bled through the armor like fire through glass. First faint, then spreading in jagged veins across his chest, shoulders, helm. Each fracture was a breath released after centuries held tight. His massive sword slipped from his hands, clanging against marble with a toll that shook the nave.

The blade itself fractured like glass and shattered.

The fractures spread through the length of the blade until it burst into a thousand shards, glittering black and crimson in the firelight, skittering across the stone before vanishing into nothing.

His armor followed after his blade. Plates cracked, splintered, fell away. Each piece dissolved before it touched the ground, curling upward into smoke and dust, leaving only a man beneath it all.

He staggered backward, each step retreating his armor falling to pieces as he stumbled towards the entrance, until he reached the broken temple doors.

A whisper faint and low across jessica's lips…*James.*

Amber eyes, no longer filled with rage, but heavy with sorrow; the kind that no words could absolve.

He looked at her, and in a voice torn ragged with ages of blood, whispered the impossible:

"Please… please forgive me."

The words tore deeper than any blade.

Jessica's chest was clenched. She wanted to speak, to tell him she could, or that she couldn't forgive him, but before she could his form began to unravel.

It wasn't sudden. It was slow. Agonizing. Grain by grain, the man and the monster crumbled away, like a statue caught in the tide, until there was nothing left.

Only the echo of his plea remained.

And Jessica's tears on the temple floor.

Chapter 26. Chains and Thunder

Jessica woke with a gasp that tore her throat raw.

The roar of flames still rang in her ears. Rome's screams twisted in her chest. The acrid scent of burning flesh clung to her memory until she pressed both hands to her face, as though she could wipe it away. But her palms came back slick with sweat, not ash.

The chamber was quiet. The red lamp on the wall dimmed as morning bled gray light through cracks in the ceiling. The silence pressed against her like a weight, the kind that follows slaughter, when even the air seems too afraid to move.

She sat cross-legged on the cot, forcing her breath into steadiness. Her fingers found her hair, dividing it into sections, weaving each strand with the mechanical calm of habit. But her mind wasn't in the present. It was still there wandering in the sand, in the blood, in the Colosseum, in the palace drenched in fire.

Rome.

And the woman. Not her, but close enough to make her chest ache. Braids tight with beads of black and white stone catching the Mediterranean sun. The same rhythm in those hands that Jessica now felt between her own fingers.

Her pulse betrayed her. She wasn't just remembering. She was *inside it*. She had been there, felt the broadsword in her grip, felt the hunger that drove him. She had been him.

She tied off the braid and let it fall over her shoulder, heart hammering in the stillness.

Fabric shifted on the far side of the room. James stepped from the wall; his hand hooked in the collar of his ruined sport coat. One shoulder was torn, a cuff smeared with dried blood, dust clinging to every fold. It looked like it had been dragged through war, because it had.

He shook his head once before peeling it off and tossing it onto the cot beside her. "Guess I'm going to need more clothes eventually," he muttered. "At this rate, I'll be down to nothing."

Jessica smirked faintly without looking up. "Not sure if that's a complaint or a promise."

A twitch pulled at his mouth, almost a smile, before his gaze caught the braid falling against her shoulder. "You always wear it like that?"

"Not always," she said, fingers already starting the next one. "Keeps it out of my face when I need to run."

"And the color… it's natural?"

She nodded. "Always had it. Born with it."

His eyes lingered longer than the question required. The silence stretched, broken only by the low growl of thunder rolling across the city, making the pipes in the walls hum. Damp air pressed heavier into the chamber, each breath carrying the scent of stone and rust. Above, rain began to patter faintly against rusted metal.

Jessica stopped braiding. Her heart wouldn't let go of the memory, the Colosseum, the fire, the slaughter. She lifted her gaze, cutting words sharper than she intended.

"So…our myths and legends of the Four Horsemen of the Apocalypse was a lie…the truth was, it was only just you?"

The words hung in the air like a blade drawn too far to be sheathed.

James met her eyes. The faint warmth was gone. Something older and heavier replaced it. "I was," he said quietly. "And I was something I grew to hate in myself."

Jessica leaned forward; forearms braced on her knees. "Is that why you were imprisoned?"

His eyes dropped, following cracks in the stone as though they might answer for him. When he spoke, his voice was softer, but not hesitant. "After Rome… I moved on from that lifetime, and wandered into another, and another. Aimless. Maybe I was looking for someone to kill me. Or something. But I found the monastery. The people there were good. Kind. They gave me what I didn't deserve. I prayed with them. Ate at their table. For a time… I knew peace."

Rain thickened above, a steady rhythm filling the silence.

"Then the angels came for me."

Jessica's head snapped up. Disbelief cut her voice. "Angels… did that to you?"

James nodded once, slow, deliberate. "When they arrived, I was leaving my sanctuary of peace to find you. The tether that connected us was pulling me. I gave up my freedom knowing I could feel you, but maybe it was best I never touch you, or the world again. I didn't fight them. Instead, I submitted to judgment. I wanted peace. But peace has a price. And mine…" his voice tightened, "…was unforgivable. They bound me in celestial chains. And I was condemned to an eternity of darkness for centuries. The monks were given a sacred charge by their bishop to protect the relics held in the chamber, unknowing to them that I was also beneath them, suffering in my solitude. In the years that passed one came down; he spoke to me through the dark. I never saw his face; he honored me by being my memory by writing everything. Every memory."

Jessica's breath caught. "All of the books. In the library. Those were your memories, it was all you?"

"Yes.", he said calmly

She brushed a braid back, pulse racing. "Then…how did I free you?"

He stepped closer. In the dim light she could see faint script etched into his skin, curling beneath his collar. celestial symbols burned into flesh. "We're connected," he said. "By my original light. That's what broke severed the chains and freed me."

Jessica frowned slightly. "Connected… like. "

"Angels are forbidden to directly interfere with the affairs of mankind," he cut her off. "It's forbidden. I was once an angel of mercy. Light. Until the Creator changed me. I was given a new purpose. Wrath became my purpose. To end the world when called. To be the creator's apocalypse to cleanse Eden."

The storm's breath thickened, humidity clinging to her skin, each inhalation tinged with iron and stone.

James's eyes softened, though his words stayed steady. "I'd seen enough savagery in this world. Then I found an innocent child. A newborn buried in the remains of a small village that was caught between two warring armies, turning the land into a battlefield, the mother already gone…" He paused, throat tightening. "I destroyed both armies to save this child. That was my sin. My exile. They stripped me from the light, bound me in mortal form, and my wings were severed. I-I…blamed humanity for my fall. I fed my rage and hatred. I then became something else."

Her voice dropped, nearly swallowed by thunder. "And you became the Horseman."

His silence was all the answer she needed.

Thunder cracked sharp and close, rattling the cot's frame. Jessica stood, tightening her satchel strap. "We may have to move soon."

James nodded, gaze rising toward the ceiling as rain hammered harder above. His voice was low, certainly.

"Yeah. The storm's coming."

He crossed to the alcove, unfastening the spout on the shower bag. Water splashed over his hands, icy and metallic. He splashed it against his face, scrubbing away the grit and dried blood. Then he pulled his shirt over his head.

Jessica froze.

Two scars ran deep down his back, pale ridges carved where wings had once been. They weren't just wounds; they were deep reminders. Burned into him by judgment itself.

Water coursed down his shoulders, across the script etched into his chest and arms. A very soft and faint golden light shimmered briefly where droplets caught the marks, like the water was waking something dormant beneath his skin.

Jessica's throat tightened. He wasn't just a man. He wasn't just a monster. He was both. And he was hers to trust. or fear.

James pressed the soap to his skin, lathering, washing with a slow, deliberate care. The faint steam that rose from him mingled with the cold air, turning the alcove into something that felt both sacred and terrifying.

For a moment, Jessica had forgot about the storm. She forgot the danger. She forgot the Reapers she didn't yet know were already moving through the city above.

All she could see was him.

Chapter 27. Dark Protocol Initiated

The rain over the city was constant now, a metallic hiss as it struck rooftops, gutters, and the black rivers running down every street. Lightning carved veins across the clouds, each flash bleaching the world into stark, ghostly whites before the darkness swallowed it again.

Far below, beneath the industrial sprawl of Hailfire Industries, the air was not wet but cold. the sterile kind of cold that burned the inside of the nose and smelled faintly of ozone and antiseptic.

Dr. Kyra Meinhardt moved through the subterranean facility like a priestess at her altar. Her black heels snapped sharply against grated flooring as she crossed from console to console, feeding in commands, locking down fail-safes she had no intention of ever using. She moved with a precision caught somewhere between urgency and reverence, as though this moment were something she had both dreaded and craved.

On the massive wall display, bold crimson letters flared into existence:

DARK PROTOCOL: INITIATED

The words pulsed like a heartbeat, their glow painting the lab in crimson strokes. Kyra let her fingers brush along the glass, as though touching the pulse of a god she had helped awaken, before turning toward the heart of the room.

Embedded into the floor was a reinforced viewport framed in steel. Beneath the ballistic glass lay the true sanctum: a sunken chamber where four colossal cryo-tubes stood in a ring. Frost rimed their armored exteriors so thick it looked carved in marble. Vapor hissed from the seams. Hydraulic lines and coolant conduits wrapped them like veins feeding a slumbering beast.

Kyra's breath fogged faintly on the glass as she leaned closer.

One tube hissed.

Then another.

The sound was slow, wet, like something reluctant being dragged back from the abyss. Steam billowed, curling against the glass in ghost-like tendrils.

Inside the chamber, two white-coated scientists moved frantically between bolted consoles, still trying to log readings, to control what could not be controlled. They had been told the subjects could not hurt them. They moved like men who half-believed it.

The frost on one capsule split in jagged lines. From within came a movement. deliberate, impossibly heavy.

A metallic fist punched through the armored door, wrenching it outward in a shriek of tortured steel. The slab of reinforced metal flew across the chamber, striking a scientist mid-torso. The man cartwheeled bonelessly into a support beam, the crack of bone sharp even over the alarms.

The second scientist screamed, sprinting for the access ladder. but he made it only three steps. Something blurred in the frost. A flash of metal. Then the wet sound of fabric tearing, the spray of arterial blood painting the walls. His body slid down the rungs, leaving a crimson trail as his lifeless hand hung limp.

The third tube groaned. Its seals burst, and the armored faceplate warped outward. A figure inside moved with sudden violence, smashing its way free. The last surviving technician scrambled into the corner, voice raw with panic, babbling prayers and begging for mercy. He barely had time to draw breath before a massive hand that was all machine and muscles closed over his skull. The sound that followed was a wet, crushing pop, silenced almost as soon as it began.

Crimson streaked the frost-glazed walls, droplets sliding upward across the ballistic glass where Kyra stood. They pooled lazily at the steel frame beneath her feet, smearing her reflection in red.

Through it all, her expression never changed. If anything, her lips curved faintly as the shapes inside stepped forward. one, then another, then all four. Shadows taller than men, armored in black composites threaded with veins of living metal. Their bodies gleamed with condensation as they tore the remnants of their prison apart, stepping onto the floor with the weight of predators reclaiming ground.

Kyra leaned closer, glasses catching the reflection of their forms. "Wonderful," she whispered, the word soft, reverent. "Simply wonderful."

Above the City

Far higher than the rain could reach, above the paths of commercial planes, three figures stood motionless against the storm. Their outlines sharpened only when lightning split the sky, silhouettes darker than the clouds themselves.

The tallest was a brute presence like a wall of stone and iron. Beside him stood another, shorter but built with the density of a siege engine, every movement promised violence. His features, when lightning struck them, were sharp and apathetic, the faint glint of ancient armor worked into his form.

Haniel.

An Archangel. A warrior forged in Heaven's oldest wars, his arrogance radiating like heat from a forge. In his eyes burned not caution but a personal hatred, one reserved for Azyrial.

The third figure moved forward into a shaft of moonlight breaking through the clouds. Her features were smooth, unreadable, her gaze cold as the rain sliding off her wings.

Ramiel.

Her voice carried clean over the storm, sounding like it had no business belonging to this world.
"He is beginning to awaken her." Soon, none of us will be able to stop him. He will become too powerful."

Haniel's lips curled faintly, almost sneering. "You underestimate me, sister. I have faced him before."

Ramiel's gaze cut sharper than the lightning. "No, brother… it is you who underestimates him. He is still absolute. Sariel, was released by him to return, there is a difference. And we mustn't forget she is the key."

The tallest figure shifted, silent, wings flexing slightly in the rain.

Haniel's voice was low, certain, every word venomous. "If he rises again, I will end him. Permanently."

Ramiel said nothing, but her silence was heavier than words. She had seen this story before. She knew how it ended.

Lightning tore across the clouds again, and in its flash their outlines vanished back into the storm.

Chapter 28. Into the Maw

The storm had moved in hard.

The streets glistened black beneath the dim glow of the streetlamps; each bulb haloed in the curtain of rain. Thunder rolled low and steady above the rooftops, its vibration rattling through the ribcages of anyone below. The air was thick with moisture, the kind that clung to skin and clothes, making every breath taste faintly of iron and wet concrete.

Inside the safehouse, the only light came from the dull red glow bleeding from the corner lamp. Jessica sat on the cot, finishing the last loop of her braid. Her fingers worked from muscle memory, each twist of hair an anchor to keep her mind from spiraling back into the memories that had opened up to her from the deep recesses of James' mind. The memory of Rome, the fire, the screams.

James stood near the door. His sport coat lay tossed onto the cot, torn and filthy, streaked with dried blood and grime. He pulled at the collar of his shirt, the button-up clinging to his frame in the humidity.

"Need to get more clothes," he muttered, half to himself. "At this rate, I'll be walking around in rags."

Jessica glanced up, a smirk tugging briefly before exhaustion stole it away. Her phone buzzed violently in her lap, the black screen flashing over and over.

She frowned and read it.

GET OUT NOW!!
THEY ARE CONVERGING!!!
DO YOU SEE THIS?!?!?!
GET OUT NOW!!!!!

The messages came in a relentless flood, the screen flashing so fast the words blurred into one another. Jessica's stomach tightened.

"James…" she said, her voice raw, urgent. "We have to go. Now."

Elsewhere

Miles away, in a basement lined with paranoia, Jessica's contact hammered keys on his jury-rigged terminal. The room was chaos. walls covered in ledgers, photographs, newspaper clippings, red twine stretching from pin to pin in frantic webs. The glow of monitors lit his sweat-slick face as streams of code raced across the screens, numbers and coordinates flashing like warnings from some dying star.

"Come on, come on…" he muttered, firing the same warning to Jessica again and again. His eyes flicked between screens, his pupils jittering, his fingers trembling from both exhaustion and adrenaline. The hum of the machines seemed louder now, oppressive, as though the building itself was straining under invisible weight.

Then he heard it.

A sound that didn't belong. A metallic clink as sharp as broken glass, cutting through the whine of fans and clicking keyboards. It echoed once, small, intimate. the sound of something dropped with intention.

His breath stopped. He turned slowly, dread crawling icy fingers up his spine.

The grenade lay at the center of the room, still spinning lazily from where it had landed. Not any grenade. He recognized it instantly. a plasma fusion core encased in thermite plating, its etched casing glowing faintly with internal charge. Four-chamber fragmentation. Kill radius: fifty feet. No survivors.

The beeping began slow, steady, patient. Then faster. Quickening into a heartbeat that filled the room. The red twine trembled on the walls from the vibration, the pinned photographs fluttering as though they wanted to flee before him.

His lips twisted into something between horror and amusement. A bitter, breathless laugh clawed its way out of his throat. "Always wanted one of those…"

For a heartbeat, the glow of his monitors lit his face and with wide eyes, sweat glistening, resignation set into the lines of his jaw. Then the grenade's light outshone everything.

White consumed the room.

Back in the Safehouse

Jessica flinched, her phone vibrating once more before the last message froze mid-word. The buzzing stopped.

The storm outside beat against the windows in pounding sheets. The boarded slats rattled in their frames.

James was already moving. Coat in one hand, his other reached for her satchel. "We're leaving. Now."

They burst out into the street, the night swallowing them immediately. Rain blurred the world into streaks of silver and shadow, headlights and neon bleeding together into a dreamlike smear. The city felt… wrong. The silence between thunderclaps pressed like a hand against Jessica's throat.

Her heart hammered. Every alley mouth looked like a set of eyes. Every rooftop felt watched.

James's grip on her hand was iron. He didn't speak, but she could feel it. the tension in his frame, the coil of a predator ready for the strike. He moved with grim precision, pulling her faster down side streets, every sense heightened.

Jessica gasped against the rain, her lungs raw from the cold air. "They're here, aren't they?"

James didn't answer. He didn't need to. She could see it in his eyes when he looked back. not fear, but recognition.

The hunt had begun.

Somewhere in the storm, something was moving with them.

Chapter 29. Prey and Predators

The rain turned the streets into black rivers. Each drop struck with the sound of static, swallowing the city in a hiss that blurred footsteps, muffled tires, erased everything except the storm itself.

Jessica's lungs burned as she ran, boots slapping waterlogged pavement. James was beside her, his hand locked around her wrist with an unrelenting grip, pulling her forward like a current. He didn't speak. He didn't need to. Every turn he chose was instinct, a predator's path through shadow and cover.

But even in the storm, Jessica could feel it. The air was wrong. Too still between the thunder. Too empty for a city this size. Every window they passed looked like an eye. Every rooftop felt watched.

Elsewhere

On the far edge of the city, in a warehouse stripped of windows, something moved.

The doors rolled back on screaming tracks, and shadows poured into the rain. A dozen shapes, uniformed in black composite armor threaded with faint veins of crimson light. Their helms were smooth, blank, no faces to meet. only slits that pulsed faintly with readouts.

They moved with the rhythm of soldiers, not men. Boots struck water in perfect unison. Weapons were cradled close, each grip deliberate, every angle precise. They were wolves set loose; their silence more menacing than the storm around them.

At their front walked the Commander. His armor carried extra plating across the chest and shoulders, and his edges were scored with marks not issued by manufacturers but by wars fought in silence. Across his breastplate, someone had etched a single jagged slash not for decoration, but a reminder.

He raised one hand. The entire unit froze.

No words. Only a series of coded pulses through their comms. each operative tilting their head faintly in response, acknowledging orders.

Then they vanished into the storm, dispersing into the city's arteries like drops of ink in water.

Back on the Streets

Jessica ducked under a flickering neon sign, dragging in a shuddering breath. Her soaked braid stuck to her back, her chest heaving. "James. " she started, but he silenced her with a look.

His amber-flecked eyes swept the street. Rain clung to his lashes, ran down the scars etched into his skin. He tilted his head, listening.

For a moment, Jessica thought he looked almost feral. not human, not angel, but something in between.

"What is it?" she whispered.

"Not the storm," he said. "Something else."

A sound broke through then. faint, almost drowned by thunder. Not footsteps. Not cars. **Boots.** Measured. Heavy. Coming closer.

Jessica's stomach tightened. She had heard that rhythm before. in training, in simulations. Soldiers. Elite ones. But these footsteps carried something worse: a patience that felt inhuman.

James pulled her toward the next alley, deeper into shadow.

"Run quieter," he murmured.

Above Them

On a rooftop across the street, two Reapers crouched. Their armor dripped with rain, crimson veins glowing faintly as they adjusted their optics. One raised a hand, signaling the others.

Through the storm, their helmets locked on two figures below: a man and a woman, moving fast.

Targets acquired.

The hunt had begun.

Chapter 30. Into the Fire

The storm had swallowed Rome whole. Rain sheeted off rooftops and hissed in the gutters, turning cobblestone streets into black rivers that erased sound. Neon bled down the walls, smeared into the monochrome of storm light.

Jessica and James tore through the alleys like fugitives chased by ghosts. Except these weren't ghosts. They were real.

From above came the rhythmic pound of boots, inhumanly precise, echoing across the rooftops. Crimson optics flickered faintly in the dark like hunting eyes. Shapes vaulted roof gaps with mechanical rhythm, sealing off streets one by one.

Jessica's lungs burned. James never slowed. His grip on her wrist was iron, pulling her forward with grim certainty.

The hunters followed and tracked them through the rain and wind with such ease. Their HUD displays relaying information quickly, and efficiently.

Through rain and shadow, their vision was sharp. The Reapers' helmets overlaid Rome in grids of tactical data: streets highlighted, targets tagged, pulses of heat shimmering through walls.

TARGETS ACQUIRED: TWO.
PRIORITY: CAPTURE.
SECONDARY: LETHAL FORCE AUTHORIZED IF RESISTANCE ESCALATES.

The Commander's voice bled into their ears. flat, calm, mechanical in tone but human beneath.

"Alpha: cut off northern exits. Bravo: herd them south. Delta: hold perimeter. No mistakes. He's not to escape."

Acknowledgments clicked back in binary tones. No chatter. No hesitation.

The First Ambush

Jessica stumbled into a wide square. and froze.

Six Reapers stood waiting, black armor gleaming wet, visors pulsing with faint crimson. Their formation was precise, cutting off every exit.

James's hand slipped from hers. He shoved her back against the wall. "Stay behind me."

Then he moved.

What Jessica saw next wasn't human.

James erupted forward in a blur, his strikes flowing like a dance: a low capoeira sweep that sent one Reaper crashing, a wall-run flip into a spinning heel kick that shattered another's shoulder. He pivoted midair, twisting into a breakspin that drove both heels into a chestplate, the impact echoing like thunder.

Jessica's eyes widened. It was chaos shaped into art. capoeira's deceptive rhythm, the elasticity of parkour, the inversions of breakdancing, sharpened by the brutal edges of gymnastics. Every motion chained into the next. It was beautiful and horrifying at once.

Armor cracked. Limbs broke. The sound of grunts, human grunts, cut through the rain.

Alerts blared across the Reapers Display

HUD ALERT: BREACH. SUIT DAMAGE DETECTED. WARNING: MULTIPLE CASUALTIES.

The Commander's voice cut in, cold and clipped.
"Do not falter. Contain him. Break him. NOW."

The Reapers surged together, pressing into formation. One caught James's arm, locking it under reinforced gauntlets. Another seized his leg, dragging him off balance.

The Reveal of Men

James's elbow drove into one Reaper's visor. The mask cracked, then shattered under the next strike. A human face spilled into view. pale, bloodied, eyes rolling in pain. He screamed.

Jessica's stomach turned.
"They're not machines," she gasped.

James grunted as another slammed him against the wall.
"Soldiers," he spat. "Altered. Controlled. But human."

The revelation hit harder than the storm.

Pinned Down

Six pressed in, overwhelming his flow. His arms wrenched behind him, his throat locked, knees driven into his ribs. Rain slicked cobblestones beneath his back. For the first time, his movements slowed.

Above him, a baton arced down, crackling with blue electricity.

Jessica lifted her weapon, heart racing. Thomas's rounds chambered like a silent promise.

One shot barked out.

A Reaper's helmet spiderwebbed and exploded, the man inside jerking back before crashing lifelessly to the stone.

The commanders HUD display light up with digital information on his current teams, relaying statistical and tactical information.

ALERT: UNITS 1, 3, 4, 5 are DOWN.
CASUALTIES REPORTED. UNIT 2 life cycles critical.

The Commander's voice was instant.
"Do not break! Adjust formation! Terminate the woman if required. HOLD HIM."

James Unleashed

The distraction was enough. James coiled like a spring and lashed out. His knee drove into a chest plate, his fists cracked another's jaw. He spun low, sweeping two off their feet, then drove an open palm into a mask, shattering it inward. The man dropped with a strangled cry.

The rest faltered, their formation collapsing.

Jessica caught her breath as James tore free, his movements sharper now. flowing, devastating, unstoppable. Armor splintered, suits failed, the air filled with the wet, breaking sounds of men caught in a dance meant for gods.

Flight Again

They staggered into the next alley, Jessica's gun still trembling in her grip. "Oh my God…" she whispered, staring at the cracked masks left behind. *Men.*

James grabbed her wrist, dragging her forward. "Don't stop now."

Boots pounded the rooftops again. Red optics flickered in the rain. Dozens of them now. More shadows dropping in from above.

The Commander's voice cut across their comms, merciless: "Phase Two. Drive them east. The Colosseum awaits."

Jessica and James vanished into the storm.

The hunt was not finished.

It had only just begun.

Chapter 31. The Blood in the Rain

The storm hammered the city like a war drum. Lightning carved scars across the sky, thunder rolled so hard it shook windows in their frames, and the streets became rivers of black water flecked with silver.

Jessica sprinted, lungs burning, boots splashing through puddles that swallowed her ankles. James was just ahead, dragging her forward with that same predatory certainty. but even he was slowing. The last fight had cost him. His shirt clung to his chest in rain and blood, and his breathing was sharper now, angrier.

And still the Reapers came.

The rooftops above were alive with them, black shapes vaulting gaps, landing heavy in the storm with the precision of machines. Crimson optics glowed through the rain like the eyes of wolves closing in on prey. The storm muffled everything except the drumbeat of their pursuit.

Jessica glanced up once, just once and nearly stumbled. Dozens of them. Maybe more. Moving in flawless formation, each leap mirrored by the next.

"James. " she gasped.

"I know." His voice was ragged, low. "Keep moving."

The Net Tightens

From somewhere unseen, the Commander's voice bled into the helmets of his soldiers. Calm. Absolute.
"Delta, cut them off. Beta, converge from the south. Phase Two: herd them east. They do not escape."

The Reapers adjusted instantly, their boots pounding rooftops in perfect rhythm. Streets narrowed; alleys began to collapse into choke points. Jessica felt the trap closing around them like jaws.

James's eyes flicked left, then right. No openings. "Here," he muttered, yanking her down a side street slick with rain.

The alley opened into a square. and they were waiting.

A dozen Reapers dropped from above, their boots slamming into cobblestones in unison, cutting off the way forward.

Jessica spun her eyes tracking movements, more behind them. They were surrounded.

Ambush Two

James shoved Jessica behind him, his chest rising and falling as he squared to the encircling pack. The storm roared around them. The red optics glowed closer.

The Commander's order rang clear in their comms.
"Engage. Subdue. Do not kill unless necessary."

Then the Reapers surged.

James exploded into motion. His body bent and twisted in impossible ways, flowing from one strike to the next in a rhythm that felt more like music than combat. He spun low, sweeping legs with capoeira rhythm, then launched into a parkour roll, using the wall to spring upward, twisting midair into a double kick that shattered two visors.

Jessica ducked low as a baton cracked sparks above her head. She fired blindly, the gunshot deafening in the enclosed square. One Reaper fell, mask cracking in spiderwebs. Another pressed in close, gauntlet raised. only for James to vault off the man's chest, flipping into a break spin that drove both heels into another's face.

The storm, the rain, the grunts of pain, it blurred together into a single violent dance.

Jessica's heart pounded. She couldn't look away. He wasn't fighting like a man. He wasn't even fighting like an angel. This was something else that seemed to have been tailored by years of fighting, an unbroken rhythm of movement and violence, beautiful and terrifying.

Overwhelmed

But the numbers were too much.

Four caught his arms at once, another locked onto his waist. One slammed a fist into his ribs. Jessica heard the crunch and winced. James roared, twisting, throwing one off, but the others clung, dragging him down like wolves pulling down a stag.

Jessica's finger tightened on her trigger. Bang. A visor cracked. Another bang. A helmet burst open, blood spraying in the rain.

The recoil numbed her hand. She whispered a silent thank you to Thomas for the new rounds. each one tearing through armor that should have been impenetrable.

James took the opening, coiling his body into a roll, snapping free, and tearing the last attacker down with a vicious elbow strike. He spun, his movements accelerating now, sharper, faster, as though the fight itself was waking something long buried.

Reaper HUD

**ALERT: MULTIPLE CASUALTIES.
UNIT COHESION COMPROMISED.**

The Commander's voice remained calm.
"Hold formation. Adjust flanks. Do not relent. Drive them to ground."

But even calm couldn't hide the edge in his tone. The man they were hunting wasn't breaking. He was growing stronger.

The Breakout

Jessica's ears rang from the gunfire. Her hands shook. James grabbed her wrist again and hauled her forward, breaking through the smallest gap in the circle. His knee shattered a Reaper's leg on the way, the man's scream ripping through the storm.

They bolted back into the alleys, splashing through rivers of rainwater, the world tilting in a blur of neon and thunder.

"James. " Jessica panted, nearly slipping. "How many are there?"

His jaw tightened. "Enough."

Boots hit rooftops above, closer now, the glow of optics following their every move. The storm no longer masked the sound. the city itself seemed to beat with the rhythm of their pursuit.

Toward the Colosseum

The Commander's voice cut in again, clipped, merciless. "Phase Three. Eastward channel complete. Surround them. The arena awaits."

And then Jessica saw it. through the sheets of rain, past the maze of alleys. the shadow of the Colosseum rising against lightning like the bones of some colossal beast.

Her breath caught.

James slowed for only a heartbeat, his amber eyes flashing with recognition.

The storm swallowed them whole again.

The hunt was not ending. It was only leading them deeper.

Chapter 32. Weight of the Watchers

The storm broke against the Colosseum like waves against a cliff. Rain cascaded down its ancient stones, pooling in the cracks carved by centuries, while thunder rolled through its hollow chambers like the growl of some buried beast.

Jessica stumbled into the arena at James's side, breath ragged, boots sliding on rain-slick stone. The moment her eyes adjusted to the massive space; her chest froze.

The Reapers were everywhere.

From above, they dropped in unison, black silhouettes descending through the storm, crimson optics glowing. From the tunnels beneath the arena, more surged out, weapons raised, forming perfect kill-box formations. Red targeting beams cut through sheets of rain, crossing over her chest, her throat, James's head.

The square of light above became a cage. There was nowhere to run.

And then he stepped forward.

The Reaper Commander.

His armor was heavier, broader than the others, every plate etched with deep scarring like claw marks. Across his back, a massive blade was sheathed, its hilt wrapped in black composite. His optics glowed brighter, deeper red than the others. His steps were deliberate, each one echoing across the soaked stone.

The storm hissed against the speakers of his helmet as his voice broke through the comms. digital, layered, chilling.
"Target acquired."

Jessica's heart hammered against her ribs. James raised his hands slowly, palms outward, body tense but controlled. His voice cut through the storm.
"Look! I'll come peacefully. She has nothing to do with this. It's me that you want, so you can let her go."

The Commander paused, tilting his head. Rain struck his armor in a sharp staccato, steaming faintly where it met the heat radiating from his frame. Slowly, deliberately, he reached back and drew the blade.

Its edge glowed red, sizzling as the storm kissed it, steam rising in thick curls. The glow painted his visor hellish.

"Those are not my orders," he said flatly. His gauntlet rose, palm forward, a gesture that could only mean one thing.
"And you are not our target."

Jessica's breath caught. She knew what was coming.

The Commander's hand lifted higher. The Reapers all shifted, weapons steadying, beams locking more tightly over them. The storm seemed to hold its breath.

And then.

They fell.

One by one, every Reaper in the arena collapsed. Weapons clattered against stone; red optics flickered out. The Commander himself staggered, blade dropping from his gauntlet, embedding into the wet floor with a hiss of steam. His massive form crashed to one knee before toppling face-first into the rain.

Silence swallowed the Colosseum.

Jessica spun, eyes wide, chest heaving.
"What the hell."

James didn't look relieved. His jaw was tight, his expression carved with something older than fear. He lifted his gaze to the storm above, to the shadows woven into the lightning.

"They're here," he murmured.

Jessica's voice cracked through the rain. "Who?"

His head snapped toward her, eyes blazing amber.
"Run! Now! Hide!!"

But it was already too late.

The storm above split open, light pouring down like fire as the heavens themselves tore into the world.

Chapter 33. The Reckoning of Brothers

Arrival of Judgment

The storm over the Colosseum was alive, a furious beast of heaven and earth. Thunder rolled in waves that shook the ancient stone, rain falling so hard it seemed like the sky itself was collapsing. The arena's floodlights cut through the storm, their harsh beams catching every sheet of water, every ripple of sand darkened to mud.

Jessica clung to James's side, heart hammering as the storm split open. Six radiant forms descended like meteors, their landing shaking the sodden ground. Wings unfurled in perfect unison, a sound like a hundred swords being drawn at once. Even the storm bowed, thunder flattening beneath the weight of their arrival.

The largest remained in the back, his presence heavier than the storm itself, his outline vast and terrible as if he was judgment incarnate.

The others gleamed in the light: one carved from onyx flesh edged with silver fire, another alabaster-white with wings feathered in steel. But Jessica's gaze was fixed on the one who stepped forward.

Haniel.

His armor was black chased with gold; each plate etched in scripture. Rain sizzled against its surface, rolling away in steaming rivulets. His wings, folded like blades, gleamed sharp enough to cut the storm. Every step he took forward was heavy with the certainty of law.

James stepped forward as well, his movements calm, his voice steady though it carried like thunder.
"Haniel."

The angel's gaze was ironed. "You disobeyed your purpose, Azyrial. You defied the Creator's command. And in doing so, you didn't just destroy yourself you condemned us all."

James's jaw clenched. "I did what I had to do. What He would not."

Haniel sneered, rain tracing the ridges of his helm. "Then bleed for it."

The Clash of Brothers

Haniel's Damascus blade came free with a hiss, flashing arcs of storm light as he struck down in a brutal overhead cut. James slipped aside, mud exploding beneath his boots, but the angel was relentless. A wing snapped outward, its steel edge cutting across James's chest. Blood sprayed, steaming where it struck the angelic metal.

Jessica gasped; the sound lost in the storm.

James countered barehanded; forearms braced against the blade's edge. Skin split, bone jarred, but he moved with centuries of instinct. He pivoted, elbow smashing into Haniel's breastplate hard enough to dent steel. The angel staggered. then smiled, rain streaking gold from the etchings of his armor.

The second assault came like a storm within the storm. Blade and wing lashed from every angle, each strike fast enough to split air and water alike. James fought like a man standing in a river of blades, flowing around strikes, redirecting the force. But Haniel pressed, merciless, each blow heavier, driving James's back across the arena floor.

Jessica's eyes widened as Haniel's wing slashed across James's back, shredding fabric, revealing the twin ragged scars where wings had once been. Old wounds, brutal and raw, carved reminders of exile.

Haniel's laughter rang like iron. "Look at you. Once radiant, chosen of the Host. Now earthbound. Wingless. Forgotten. You will never be forgiven. Never rise again."

Rain plastered James's shirt to his skin, the blood from fresh wounds mixing with the stormwater until it ran in ribbons down his body. Jessica's throat locked as she saw the scars, the place where something holy had been ripped away. Her hands trembled at her sides. She wanted to move, to cry out, to throw herself between them. but she could not.

The storm drowned her voice, and the weight of the fight pressed her into silence. All she could do was watch, heart breaking with each strike that landed, each fresh ribbon of blood carved into him.

An Angel's Hatred

Haniel pressed forward again, a blade carving across James's ribs, wing cracking against his side. James staggered, catching himself, then surged forward, driving his head into the angel's helm. Sparks erupted as steel cracked against steel. Haniel faltered but only for a breath before slamming a wing across James's chest, throwing him back into the sodden ground.

Jessica screamed his name, but the storm swallowed it whole. James dragged himself up, blood coursing down his chest, mud caking his hands. He rose slowly, shoulders squared, as Haniel's blade came gleaming overhead.

"This ends now," Haniel spat, rain hissing on his steel.

James twisted under the swing, catching the angel's arm and wrenching until the joint snapped with a sickening pop. The Damascus blade fell, clattering to the stone. James caught it, his eyes burning amber as he pressed it to Haniel's throat.

"End it!" Haniel roared, defiance spitting blood from his lips.

For a heartbeat, James hesitated. the storm holding its breath. Then his rage broke. With a roar, he drove the blade through Haniel's chest, pinning him to the floor of the arena.

The sound was bone and thunder. Haniel's scream ripped through the heavens as his body burst into blinding light. Shards of brilliance scattered upward into the storm; streaks of fire swallowed by the black sky.

The rain itself seemed to recoil, hissing as if it touched the holy light.

James staggered back, shirt shredded, ribs bleeding. The scars across his back glistened in the storm light, wounds of flesh and spirit both.

From the shadows at the arena's edge, the towering figure stepped forward at last. Lightning licked across his armor, thunder carrying his voice as if the storm itself bent to him.

"You have taken the light of one of our own, Azyrial. You cannot escape the Creator's judgment. And neither will she. This is His command."

Jessica froze; chest tight as steel pressed to her throat. The words were more than threat. they were a decree.

The angels spread their wings, one by one ascending in arcs of fire and light until only two remained: the towering figure and Ramiel.

Ramiel's gaze lingered on James, unreadable. Then, almost imperceptibly, she bowed her head. Not submission. acknowledgment. Respect. James dipped his head in return, blood mixing with rain down his face.

Then she was gone. Only Michael's pronouncement lingered in the storm.

Into the Catacombs

The arena fell quiet but heavier, the storm was muted by the absence of wings.

James turned, his voice hoarse. "We can't stay. The streets will be worse."

Jessica followed him through broken archways, into collapsed ruins at the far end of the Colosseum. They ducked into the yawning black of the catacombs.

The storm's roar dimmed above. The air grew cooler, damp, thick with the smell of limestone and centuries of dust. Their flashlights cut thin paths across walls stacked with skulls, the empty sockets following them. Every footstep echoed too loud, bouncing down endless tunnels.

James leaned heavily against the stone, shirt in tatters, blood dripping steadily. Jessica's light trembled as it passed over his back. the twin scars raw and brutal, carved deeper than flesh.

The Weight of His Scars

"Sit," Jessica whispered. "Just... sit."

He lowered himself onto a block of stones, rain and blood running together down his arms. He hunched forward; hair plastered to his face.

Jessica moved before she thought. Her fingertips brushed one scar, tracing the jagged ridge. James flinched but didn't pull away.

"You don't have to. " he began.

"I know," she said softly. Her hand pressed flat over both scars, steady. "But I want to."

His breath caught. For a long moment, the storm above was only a memory. "It always hurts. Not the flesh. The memory."

Her hand pressed firmer, grounding him. "They wanted this to mark you forever. To make you remember only what you lost. But it doesn't make you less. Not to me."

His amber eyes dimmed, sorrow etched deep, but something softer flickered in the dark. a smile, faint and worn, but real.

Forward

For a time, they sat in silence, the only sound the drip of water somewhere in the dark. Then a metallic clang echoed down the tunnels, distant but closing.

James pushed himself up with her help. His voice was low, steady. "They're moving again. We can't stay."

Jessica caught his hand, holding it tight. "Then we move together."

They descended deeper into the catacombs, swallowed by darkness. The storm rumbled faint above, but between them lay something unspoken, a bond born in blood and scars, stronger than judgment, stronger than heaven or hell.

And nothing was going to sever it.

Chapter 34. They Came from the Shadows

A Breath Before the Storm

The catacombs breathed around them like a sleeping beast. Damp air clung to the stone, carrying the taste of rust and bones long since turned to dust. The storm outside was a faint, muffled growl through the earth, thunder like the distant pacing of a predator waiting its turn.

Jessica kept close behind James, her flashlight beam jittering along rows of skulls stacked in endless alcoves. She could hear his breathing, steady and deep, but felt the tension radiating off him like heat.

Finally, he stopped at a cracked pillar, leaning into it, one hand pressed to his ribs.

Jessica crouched, angling the light across his torn shirt. The wounds along his chest and back glistened red, the scars where wings had once been ragged and cruel. She reached out, tracing the ridges with her fingertips.

He flinched, but she didn't pull back.
"They didn't break you," she whispered. "Not then. Not now."

His jaw clenched. "You don't know what I've done. What I became."

"I don't care," she said, steady. Her hand spread across his back, covering the scars like a seal. "What I saw in that arena… you didn't fight to destroy. You fought to survive. And to protect me."

For a heartbeat, his eyes softened, a glow of amber dimmed by weariness. He closed his hand over hers, rough and calloused but trembling.
"You shouldn't be near me, Jessica. I'll only drag you down."

"Then I'll go down with you."

Silence pressed between them. not hollow, but heavy, alive with something neither could name.

Then the silence shifted.

The drip of water that had been echoing ahead was gone. The air grew thick, still, heavy with the scent of ozone.

James stiffened. His head lifted, amber eyes narrowing.
"They're here."

The Ghost That Walks

It came without warning.

A blur of motion tore through the dark, too fast for Jessica's light to catch. Sparks erupted from the stone wall, twin blades carving deep grooves into ancient limestone.

Jessica spun, pistol snapping up just as the figure emerged fully into her beam.

Black armor sculpted for speed, curved blades like liquid metal catching the light. The Phantom of the Dark Protocol.

Dagan.

He moved with surgical precision. His first strike wasn't aimed at her chest, but her weapon. One impossibly exact cut split the bullet already chambered. and severed the barrel clean off. The ruined gun clattered against the wall.

Jessica staggered back, gasping. *My only gun.*

The second blade whistled toward James, catching across his sternum. Flesh tore, blood spattered the stone.

James roared and slammed forward, his heel crashing into Dagan's chest plate hard enough to rattle the tunnel. The assassin skidded back, but landed fluidly, blades spinning in a blur.

Then the swarm arrived.

The Reapers Swarm

Shadows moved in the side corridors, heavy boots striking stone. Dozens of armored figures emerged, matte-black plating etched with faint crimson lines. Their helmets glowed with pulsing red optics, synchronized in time.

Reapers.

Jessica scrambled back, her destroyed weapon clattering at her feet. She was unarmed. Helpless.

"Jessica!" James shouted but was already engulfed.

He met them head-on. His body flowed in a storm of violence. capoeira spins whipping his heels into helmets, parkour leaps carrying him up the walls and crashing down on armored shoulders, break-spin kicks snapping spines. Every strike was surgical, every movement woven from centuries of combat.

Jessica's chest seized. this wasn't the nightmare Horseman she'd seen in her visions. This was something else. Controlled chaos. Precision violence. He wasn't killing. not when he could avoid it. He was dismantling them, breaking limbs, smashing armor until human faces stared back through shattered masks.

But there were too many. For everyone that fell, two more pressed in. Their hive-tactics weren't elegant, but they didn't need to be. They just needed to keep him busy.

And they did.

It's A Trap

Jessica backed into a narrow corridor, heart hammering. Her hands scrambled over her satchel for anything. a knife, anything. when the shadows behind her moved.

A shape larger than any Reaper stepped from the dark. Massive. Brutal. Servo-muscles whined beneath heavy armor, every step shaking the stones.

Orc.

She spun, but it was too late. His arms locked around her like steel girders.

The discharge hit instantly.

White-blue lightning arced across her body, every nerve alight with pain. She screamed, the sound jagged against the stone, before her legs buckled. Smoke curled from her clothes as her body sagged against his grip.

"Jessica!" James roared, breaking three Reapers with his bare hands, blood and armor spraying. He sprinted toward her.

But Dagan was there. The Phantom blurred in, blades flashing, forcing James's back with a storm of slashes. Sparks lit the dark, steel screaming against bone and muscle.

Jessica's vision blurred, her head dropping forward. Orc lifted her effortlessly, disappearing into the shadows.

My Heart Was Taken

James exploded through the last of the Reapers, blood streaming down his chest. He lunged into the open air just as Orc shimmered into the night, Jessica's limp body in his arms.

Above, a dropship hovered. whisper-quiet, antigravs glowing faint blue against the rain.

"Jessica!!" James screamed, raw and hoarse.

The ship rose into the storm, engines flaring. Wind tore at him, rain lashing his face, plastering his shirt to his back until the scars carved there stood out like brands. His fists clenched, muscles trembling with fury as he stumbled forward into the downpour.

But the ship was already gone. swallowed by thunder.

He fell to his knees, screaming her name until the storm drowned him out.

The Predator's Touch

Jessica's eyes fluttered open to red light.

Her body jerked weakly against restraints that bit into her skin, nerves still twitching from whatever voltage had slammed her under. Every muscle felt heavy, locked in place, refusing to obey. Her throat was raw, her chest heaving shallowly as if each breath was rationed by the machine that bound her.

She was upright, pinned inside a standing frame. Carbon-steel clamps pressed across her wrists, her chest, her waist, cruelly precise. built for prisoners, not people. The cold bit through her skin, locking her into stillness.

The dropship thrummed around her, a constant mechanical heartbeat. Red strobes pulsed along the bulkhead in intervals, bathing the compartment in light that resembled fresh blood. The smell was wrong. ozone, scorched oil, and something coppery that had seeped into the seams of the ship long ago.

Then she heard it.

Movement.

A scrape down the metal wall. talons dragging slowly, deliberately, not to test the steel but to announce themselves.

From the shadows, she emerged.

Yaga.

Her armor caught the red light in jagged fragments: matte black plating, segmented and tight across her form like the exoskeleton of some engineered predator. The plates whispered and clicked with each step, as if the suit itself breathed with her. A black scarf wound around her throat and helm, one strip trailing loosely behind her head. It twitched with each movement like a serpent's tongue, alive and hunting.

The helm concealed everything. Smooth, faceless, sharp in its edges. No eyes, no expression. Jessica could not read her. only feel the cold void pouring from that visor.

Yaga stopped inches away.

One armored arm rose, talons bracing against the wall beside Jessica's head. The metal groaned under her weight. With the other, she reached up, gauntlet claws tilting Jessica's chin. Cold steel traced her jawline. The pressure wasn't piercing, but it was enough to let her know the talons could sink in whenever Yaga chose.

Jessica turned her face sharply, forcing a defiant edge into her fear.
"Don't you fucking touch me."

The helmet tilted, birdlike, predator curious. A low chuckle rasped through the voice modulator, distorted and venomous. "Oh…" Yaga's voice dripped slow, deliberate, like poison. "…I'll do more than touch you."

The talons dragged downward, pressing hard into Jessica's chest until the air fled her lungs. She gasped, fighting for breath, but Yaga leaned in closer, helm almost brushing her cheek. The scarf brushed Jessica's shoulder. a cold, alien caress, like a predator marking its prey.

The vox dropped to a whisper.
"When we're finished, we'll carve every soft piece of flesh from your body. Piece by piece, I'll savor cutting your fucking heart out myself bitch. And when your protector is finally ours…" The helm turned slightly, predator-like. "…I'll feed it to him."

Jessica strained against the frame, a deep fury boiling through her helplessness. Her body trembled with the effort, but the steel refused to give. The more she resisted, the deeper Yaga pressed, talons biting cruelly against her ribs.

Yaga tilted her helm as if listening. savoring the rhythm of Jessica's racing heartbeat. Her chuckle rumbled low, guttural, vibrating like a growl inside the armor.
"Good. You have a fight in you. It makes the breaking… so much sweeter."

Jessica spat words back through clenched teeth. "You'll never break me."

Yaga leaned in, visor inches from Jessica's eyes. Though faceless, the weight of her stare pressed like fangs sinking into flesh.
"They all say that."

The strobes on Yaga's arms flared open. And the electrodes lit.

Pain detonated through Jessica's body. White-hot, merciless. Every nerve caught fire at once, every muscle convulsing as if tearing from her bones. Her scream split the dropship's silence, raw and ragged, until it dissolved into choking gasps.

Yaga stayed close. Watching. The talons traced her cheek again, almost gentle now, a parody of tenderness.

Jessica's scream faltered. Her head sagged forward, chin dropping to her chest, hair clinging to damp skin. The restraints hissed as they adjusted, holding her limp body upright.

The world collapsed into black.

The last thing she heard before the void swallowed her was Yaga's whisper, low and satisfied, curling like smoke around her mind:

"You'll beg before the end. They all do."

END BOOK I

The past refuses to stay buried.

Jessica is haunted by fragments of lives she cannot explain. Visions of battlefields, ancient cities, and a love that spans centuries stalk her waking hours. Each memory pulls her closer to a truth she was never meant to uncover and to the man bound to her by fire and eternity.

James, once a weapon of judgment, now walks the world broken and relentless. For centuries he has searched for the one soul who could unmake him or save him. That search ends with Jessica.

Shadows are closing in. Angels, demons, and powers older than heaven itself move against them. As Jessica is drawn into a war she cannot escape, she must decide whether the man she is bound to is her salvation or the beginning of her end.

Horseman Book II Ashes of Constant

Chapter 1. Descent Into Hailfire

The dropship lived in her bones.

It wasn't just the hum. though that was there, a low, constant pressure that vibrated through metal and tendon. it was the *pulse* of the thing. The deck plates picked it up and fed it into Jessica's feet, into the cuffs, into her aching shoulders until her own heartbeat tried to keep time with it and failed.

She hung upright in the restraint frame, wrists pinned high, ankles locked tight. The extension had reached a place past pain and into something hollow and electric; her fingertips tingled, her biceps burned, and the joints in her shoulders ached with hot, glassy insistence. Every breath scraped the back of her throat raw. The cabin lights strobed a surgical red that washed the interior like a cauterized wound. on, off, on. too slow to be a warning, too steady to be mercy.

The air tasted like ozone and old metal. Under it, a thinner note of hydraulic oil. The ship was warm in the way machines are warm. exhaust breath, not body heat. yet sweat beaded at her temples and ran in thin, salty lines into her hairline. A drip from the ceiling struck the side of her neck and crawled cold under the collar of her shirt. She flinched without meaning to, the motion tugging fire through her shoulders again.

A kiss of static. Then the magnetic locks **snapped**.

The frame released with a pair of crisp clacks, more felt than heard, and gravity had her. Her arms dropped. Blood surged back into numbed nerves like a flood through narrow pipes. Needles bloomed up her forearms so bright she almost retched. Her cuffed hands thumped against her stomach; her knees wobbled.

Two figures moved in the red. Reapers. matte-black armor with faint crimson tracery that pulsed like sleeping veins. They closed on her with the economy of tools, gauntlets sliding under her elbows, grips tightening hard enough to bruise and then tighter. She twisted on instinct. just a shrug and a wrench to make space, to remember she could. but the motion barely existed before the consequence did.

A third hand came from behind and *took* the back of her neck.

Not fingers. A clamp. Pressure ratcheted up with the whine of a micro-servo. Pain should have climbed; instead, it **jumped**. Heat spiked down her spine and bloomed outward in a white, scalding sheet that made her jaw lock and her vision spark at the edges. Her head snapped back until her teeth clicked.

A voice slid into her ear, feminine and synthetic, the modulator smoothing cruelty into something silken.

"Be compliant," it said, breath a cold fan across her skin, "or I'll begin carving you here and now, *bitch*."

Yaga.

The clamp was released. The pain didn't. It stored itself in muscle and nerve, a phantom hand that stayed long after it was gone. Jessica swallowed hard against the bile taste rising in her mouth and forced a breath in, then out. *Count. Four in, six out.* The numbers were threads; she tried to hold on to them the way she once held on to yarn, letting them slip between mental fingers and catch, make a pattern, make anything that wasn't just naked fear.

The dropship banked. Her stomach fell sideways. Through a narrow, rain-streaked viewport, the storm broke long enough to sketch the city in lightning: slabs of glass, knife-edges of steel, signage blinking ink-blue and gold. And rising from the black water like a blade meant to cut the sky. **the Citadel**. Obsidian faces. Gold veins running its spine as if something inside it beat. For a breath, the tower seemed to swallow the lightning instead of reflecting it.

The hum deepened. Auto-gyros sang. The ship slid into a silent glide and nosed toward a mouth opening near the tower's base. a skylift dock, rimmed in running lights that turned the rain to falling wires. Magnetic grapples **thunked** onto the hull. Pressure equalized with a soft hiss that felt like a sigh against her eardrums.

The ramp began to descend.

Air rolled in. cold and metallic, antiseptic threaded through it until her eyes watered. The new smell layered over the old: clean in the way of things that had been sterilized so many times the cleanliness felt poisonous. Beneath it, the faint sweetness of coolant and the iron breath of wet steel.

The floor beyond wasn't just busy; it was *alive*. Jessica felt the difference before she saw it. The deck under the ramp pulsed. *thrum-thrum*. as if the tower had a heart somewhere in its depths and the blood ran up through its bones. The sound map of the bay sharpened: the hard drum of boots on metal, syncopated and exact; the buzz of drone-gnats flitting under the rafters; the low, omnipresent whir of power moving through conduits in the walls.

Voices, too, but kept clipped and low, anti-echo speech that sounded like code more than talk.

Uniformed soldiers in stone-gray moved in clean chevrons, rifles crossed against chests, and opaque visors. Scientists in pale coats threaded between them, eyes on tablets, lips moving just enough to count or name. Each had a lanyard with a flashing tag; the colors changed in sequence, making a rhythm Jessica's brain tried to solve and couldn't.

They shoved her forward. The ramp's metal ridges bit through the thin soles of her boots. Her cuffed hands were heavy now that they had nowhere to go. A tremor ran through them she couldn't away. She pressed her tongue to the roof of her mouth to stop the click of her teeth and tasted copper again.

At the foot of the ramp stood a woman who might have been sculpted out of precision: **Dr. Kyra Meinhardt**. Charcoal coat tailored tight across the shoulders; hair braided so neatly it looked like it inked onto her skull. She held a tablet like an altar offering and wrote without looking up, the stylus whispering across glass. The glare from the screen lit the bottom half of her face and left her eyes in cool shadow until she turned the slightest degree and they caught light, gray, measuring.

"Subject arrives alert," she said to the tablet, voice uninflected. "Visible tremor. Pupils reactive. Residual neuromuscular response from electro-discharge. Skin clammy. Respiration elevated. Note: stress response high even for. "

Her gaze flicked up, took Jessica in. sweat, cuff-bruises blooming purple, the way she held herself on the edge of collapse and refusal. The stylus wrote two more words that Kyra didn't bother to speak aloud. Jessica couldn't see them. She didn't need to.

The ramp shivered.

Something vast moved behind her. The deck underfoot vibrated with a deeper register, a grinding bass that made the fillings in her teeth itch. Servo-muscles wine-sawing through weight. Armor scraping armor.

She didn't want to turn. She did anyway.

Orc filled the dropship's mouth.

He stepped out like a piece of the tower had learned to walk. thickness on thickness, slabs of armor layered over musculature too big to be human. Gyros in his calves hummed as he planted, each step settling with the impact of piledrivers, the deck flexing and then accepting him like a thing it had been built to carry. His helm was a blunt wedge with no face, only the narrow glow of buried optics like coals seen through ash.

Heat came off him in waves. not fever heat, not life heat. Engine heat.

Jessica's lungs forgot how to do their job. The world tunneled down to a circle and then another. Her skin became cold and tight. *Don't. Don't fold. Breathe.* She tried. Air went in and hit a wall in her chest and came back out as a thin animal sound between her teeth.

Up close, his armor told truths she didn't want to know. Parts of his armor had anchor ports recessed along the shoulder carapace and spine, shock absorbers and lock points machined to tolerances so fine they looked organic. Places for Yaga to set her clamps. Places for a rifle to seat so recoil never mattered. He wasn't built to be a man. He was built to be a **stabilization platform**.

A soft rasp of fabric on armor sounded behind her right ear; Yaga had come down the ramp too. Jessica didn't look. She could *feel* the cold attention pass over her like a scanner beam, the way the modulator's faint hiss tinted the air when Yaga breathed. The soft sway of a scarf in conditioned wind.

The Reapers corrected their grips when Jessica's knees dipped. one fraction too much slack, one fraction too much resistance, and the gauntlets recalibrated. The precision made her stomach lurch. She focused on a scuff mark near her left boot. toe-sized, crescent-shaped, oil-dark at the edge. because it was a thing made by a person who had once been rushed or careless and that meant people *could* be both in here, even if the place pretended otherwise.

"Proceed," Dr. Kyra said, not looking away from her screen.

The closest Reaper angled Jessica toward the bay. The temperature changed as they crossed the threshold. cooler a few degrees, dryer, the air-processing units up in the rafters sighing a steady respiratory sound. Overhead, a crane crawled along a rail the way an insect moved along a vein. The floor's pulse picked up under her boots, or maybe her heart did; it was impossible to tell which belonged to her and which belonged to the Citadel.

They passed a row of glass-walled rooms that weren't rooms so much as instrument frames and gantries and tables with restraints disguised as ergonomics, imaging arrays that threw grids of light over anything placed inside them. The glass wore a fog of handprints at human height that someone had tried to wipe away and hadn't managed. The smear pattern made a shape her mind didn't want to assemble. She looked down again.

Her mouth had dried to papery paste. She worked her tongue against her teeth and tasted nothing. The chemical brightness in the air lapped at the back of her throat and made her eyes sting. She let them. Better that than the hot blur that wanted out.

"Vitals stable," Kyra's voice said somewhere behind, transcribing to glass. "Elevated cortisol. Non-compliant response to restraint. expected. Begin intake."

You are not prey, Jessica told herself, but the thought had no weight. It felt like saying *you are not drowning* while water climbed past your mouth.

They marched her off the ramp and into the flight bay properly. The space swallowed sound the way snow does, muting shouts into tight, functional syllables. Motion was everywhere but it had no edges; nobody bumped into anyone else, nobody crossed anyone else's lines. She felt conspicuous and invisible at the same time cataloged from a dozen angles by cameras she couldn't see, forgotten by any eye that remembered mercy.

Her breath hitched again when Orc's shadow crossed her path, blotting the red light, replacing it with a heavier dark. He moved past with Yaga pacing him. predators in tandem: the hammer and the needle. She stared at the seam where two deck plates met and tried to count the tiny hex screws. One, two, three. The numbers broke apart and scattered.

The Reapers turned her toward a door. It irised open like a pupil. Cold air pooled out of it across her shins. Inside, the light went from red to white, from threat to clinical, and the smell shifted with it. less oil, more antiseptic, a note of something sweet and wrong under both, like fruit left too long in an engine room.

Jessica's shoulders throbbed as if the frame still held her. Her cuffs were heavy as anchors. Fear had moved from her head into her hands, a tremor she couldn't still; she pressed her wrists together to hide it and the metal bit bone.

She glanced back once, because her FBI training taught her to visually take notes of everything around her.

The ramp was already coming up. The enclosed bay ate the ship. The Citadel blinked. one long, slow pulse of its hidden heart. and in the echo of it she felt a different thrum, distant and thin, somewhere far beyond the storm and steel.

James, she thought, and the thought steadied for a beat. *Find me.*

The door was sealed. The hum grew closer. The tower took her in.

www.ingramcontent.com/pod-product-compliance
Lightning Source LLC
Chambersburg PA
CBHW020237120726
47903CB00008B/2708